Lone Wolf

This is a work of fiction. Similarities to real people, places, or events are entirely coincidental.
LONE WOLF
First edition: February 29th, 2020
Copyright © 2020 Kristin Coley
Written by Kristin Coley

Chapter One

Caleb

Cautiously, I scouted the area, Trent's warnings ringing in my ears. It was slow going with dense underbrush roughly catching against my jeans, but I knew better than to shift. I'd narrowly avoided a rusty trap hidden in a shallow ravine when I'd crossed onto their lands. There was no telling what else lurked in the shadowed forest of the Ghost Pack.

A glimmer of sunlight trickled through the canopy and I straightened to my full height as I found myself in a clearing. I inhaled deeply, but was once again disappointed. No scents lingered here, almost as if the forest was devoid of life and I wondered if the wolf pack we'd dubbed the Ghosts had abandoned the area.

I glanced around, the silent forest eerie in the middle of the day. Not a single bird or animal moved, reinforcing the idea that nothing but ghosts lived here. My gaze skimmed the surrounding trees, alert to anything that would indicate someone had been there at some point.

My eyes caught on a vertical line scarring the trunk of a tree. It might have been natural, but instinct prodded me to look closer. I walked slowly, my gaze sweeping the forest floor, and I froze as my boot hit something buried under the leaves. The dull ring of metal hitting metal echoed loudly as the trap snapped shut, and I took a steading breath as I eased my foot back.

I carefully crouched down, using a stick to brush away the leaves that hid the trap from view. Shiny metal gleamed in the dim light that filtered through the heavy canopy above, and a sharp hiss escaped me. Someone was definitely still here.

I lifted my head slowly and scanned the area again, this time careful to note anything out of place. A single broken branch caught my eye and I exhaled. It was about the right height for a small wolf, *a young one or perhaps a female*, I judged.

"What are you keeping out?" I wondered aloud, my voice almost deafening in the quiet clearing. I ran my finger over the vertical line someone had intentionally carved into the tree and then back down at the trap I'd just accidentally sprung. "Or maybe, what are you trying to keep in?"

I glanced back the way I'd come, obligation tugging at me to go back, knowing Dom would approve of that course of action, but a decade old curiosity wouldn't let me. I'd wanted to know more about this Pack since I'd first learned of them, and Trent's mysterious interaction with them had only intensified the desire. It had taken me years to finally get here, and I had no intention of leaving without some answers.

***

I trudged forward, growing careless in the fading light as I continued to find nothing, not even a hint of life in the rapidly darkening forest. I either had to turn back or make camp, and I was leery to remain on another Pack's land without invitation.

You shouldn't be here.

I froze as the words seemed to whisper on the wind, except not a single leaf stirred.

Go.

I remained still, but my gaze swept the area, trying to find who or *what* had spoken.

Leave and never return.

I licked my lips, fighting the urge to run like hell as the words screamed through my mind, tearing at my sanity as they evoked a fear unlike anything I'd ever felt.

"It's not real," I chanted softly, locking my knees when they threatened to give out. Everything about this place was unnatural and my wolf whined pathetically. I knew if I'd been in my wolf form, I would have run without looking back.

I forced myself to move forward, alert once more as I fought through the fear fogging my brain. After a few steps it seemed to lessen and I stepped forward eagerly.

Too eagerly.

Serrated teeth tore through flesh as they snapped bone and blood filled my mouth. I fell to the ground as the trap locked against my leg, teeth clenched to silence the scream that threatened to escape. I lay panting on the ground, each exhale loud in the once again silent forest. I inhaled through my nose, controlling my breathing as I fought the pain, knowing I couldn't afford to pass out.

My only chance was to spring the trap, something I couldn't do as a wolf, which meant I had to control my natural inclination to shift and heal my shredded leg.

I inched forward, trying not to move my leg as each pulsing throb of pain pushed me closer to passing out. My fingers brushed metal and I closed my eyes in relief. I traced the razor sharp grooves of the trap, following them down to find the release mechanism.

A flicker in the trees caused me to hesitate and I scanned the area as I wondered if I'd imagined the movement. I fumbled with the spring, sudden urgency driving me as my fingers slipped on the blood coating the metal. I was a sitting duck and it was clear that whatever haunted these woods didn't want me here.

My thumb found the pin and with a screech the metal teeth entrapping me released. I yanked my foot free, scrambling backwards on my butt as white fur flashed, a beacon in the gathering darkness.

My back hit a tree and I considered shifting into my wolf form, but my leg was broken and without setting it first, I risked permanent damage.

I inhaled, trying to get something, anything, on whatever was circling me, but not a single trace drifted on the still air, nothing but the coppery scent of my own blood.

You should have run when you had the chance.

The light voice almost sang, chiding me, and I blinked. It was a human voice, spinning merrily on a nonexistent wind, and only I seemed to hear it as a black and white wolf lunged from the deepening shadows, teeth gleaming as they locked onto my throat in a death grip.

Chapter Two

Caleb

"It's time to come home." My shoulders curved as Dom's words settled over me heavily. It wasn't a command….yet. But how could I tell him that the place he called home had never felt that way to me? That after years of wandering I still hadn't found that elusive thing he'd found with Jess. I clutched the phone in my hand, taking a deep breath, as I fought the urge to argue. My silence seemed to echo on the line and I heard him exhale. "We're worried."

We…..always we. I scratched my eyebrow, hating the bitterness I felt, but understanding *why* didn't change anything. Jess's appearance in our lives had changed everything, including my friendship with Dom, and my own envy over their relationship didn't help matters.

"I know," I muttered, knowing he needed something from me. "It's just –"

"Just what?" Dom interrupted tiredly. "There's always an excuse, Caleb. Some reason you can't come home, and I admit I don't understand. Help me understand."

I closed my eyes, wishing I could.

"You haven't seen the kids in *years*. When was the last time you ran with a Pack?"

Did running from a lynch mob count?

I bit back the automatic response, knowing it would cause Dom to order me home immediately and I wouldn't be able to ignore an Alpha directive. "It's been awhile. But I'm good," I reassured him and he scoffed.

"Jess wants to know if you're eating," he said instead of lecturing me, and involuntarily I smiled. "She says send a picture because she won't believe you otherwise."

"I can do that," I replied quickly, sensing a reprieve. Dom didn't speak for so long I wondered if we'd been disconnected. I glanced at the phone screen but the call was still active.

"Do you want to form your own Pack?"

The question was so unexpected I sat back on my haunches, stunned.

"Is that the reason you won't come home?" He sighed as I tried to figure out how to respond. "You can tell me, Caleb. I won't judge. You were Alpha and I forced you into my Pack."

"No," I managed to blurt out. "No, Dom. That's nothing…..no."

"Caleb, I would understand."

"I know you would," I burst out. "But that's not why. I appreciate what you did. You saved my life that night. I can never repay that, not in a hundred lifetimes." He must have heard the truth in my voice because he grunted. "I'll come home, just…not yet," I gritted out, not wanting to admit how close I actually was to home.

"I don't like that we need a phone to communicate," he growled in frustration and I grimaced. "Lone wolves don't….they don't do well, Caleb."

"Good thing I'm not a lone wolf then, isn't it?" I joked, but it fell flat as he remained silent. "I swear I'm fine and I'll send a picture as soon as I hang up. I'll be back on Pack lands before you know it." I glanced at the edge of the border between Navarre Pack lands and the Ghost Pack. I was at the extreme northern edge of the border, at a crossroads that had once been Hanley land until Dom had taken them over. One step to the right and technically I would be standing on Pack land, but I didn't move.

"Fine, but you check in."

"No problem," I agreed, relief filling me.

"Every day."

That was a problem. "Weekly?"

"Every. Single. Day." His tone brooked no argument and I swallowed my automatic argument. "I mean it, Caleb. You miss a check in and I'll come find you."

I believed him and knowing Jess, she'd be right there with him.

"I'll check in," I promised, crossing my fingers behind my back even though he couldn't see me. An angry scream cut across the line and Dom muttered something unintelligible.

"I have to go," he spoke over the sound of crying and I ignored a familiar pang in my chest. "One of the kids just broke something. Hopefully not another kid. Check in," he finished, the order clear as the line went dead.

I waited a second and then hit another number in my phone.

Trent picked up almost immediately, greeting me almost fondly. "To what do I owe the pleasure of a call from the proverbial lone wolf?"

"Tell me again about the Ghost Pack," I answered, making myself comfortable on the hard ground.

Chapter Three

Caleb

*She **hates** intruders.*

The blithe words barely registered as the wolf above me growled, the sound reverberating through my chest as the she wolf's teeth tightened on my throat.

Good to know, I thought distantly and was rewarded with surprised laughter.

***You**, I like*, the voice decided, sounding faintly disappointed as it added, *too bad you're going to die.*

Thanks, I managed to reply as I decided to risk the shift, catching the female pinning me to the ground off guard as my shape suddenly changed and she was forced to rebalance.

Her scent surged through me the second I shifted into my wolf form and I staggered. She pounced instantly, going for my throat again, and I brought my head down, snarling. She paused, clearly assessing how much of a threat I was now that we were more evenly matched.

You're a wolf? The astonished question echoed through my brain and I fought the urge to glance around to find whoever was blasting thoughts through my mind with the ease of a Pack mate.

You couldn't tell? I grunted, keeping a wary eye on the female sizing me up.

Well, no. The voice suddenly sounded uncertain and young, distracting me just long enough for her to attack.

Her teeth snapped entirely too close to my throat and I rolled her, using my heavier weight to pin her to the ground, grateful she wasn't in heat as she struggled to buck me off.

Stop, I roared in frustration as her scent threatened to take me down. It took a second to realize she'd stopped moving and suddenly I wondered if she was the voice I'd been hearing.

Nope, a now familiar voice piped up, and sensing my relief, quickly ruined it. *She's my sister.*

The wolf under me snarled and I raised up slightly, taking some of my weight off her. She immediately tried to escape and I slammed back down, hearing her breath whoosh out of her.

Be still, I barked mentally and felt more than heard her growl at the command. She hadn't spoken to me telepathically, but she seemed to understand me just fine.

Care to explain? I asked tiredly, certain I'd lost my mind somewhere in this unnatural forest. I was communicating telepathically with an unknown female, which should have been impossible since she wasn't Pack, and the wolf I'd pinned seemed to understand me.

Explain what? The same voice chirped, confusion marring her voice.

Our strangeness, another voice snarled, snapping my attention back to the wolf under me as she pulled my trick and shifted. The white wolf disappeared and in her place was a striking woman.

"Now, *get off*, you foolish idiot," she snapped, her fingers burying into my thick coat as she shoved at my chest, sharp nails digging as her eyes flashed a warning. I quickly rolled off of her, shifting back into my human form. I stood, hiding a grimace as my leg protested. The break hadn't healed properly and I didn't need to look down to know a scar had formed on my flesh.

She raked her gaze over me, not bothering to play at modesty and I stood silent, letting her look. The scar across my chest had faded over the last decade but there was no mistaking it had been a killing wound. An Alpha fight only had one outcome but thanks to Dom, I'd been the exception. Her eyebrow lifted as she came to my privates and I had a sudden urge to cup them protectively. Her gaze continued and I felt as much as heard her sigh when she saw my leg.

"Are you sure it's a wolf?" She muttered under her breath and I snorted.

"Would you like another demonstration?" I retorted, catching the smallest twitch of her lip before she resumed her blank expression. "Or perhaps you're the one who is unclear on the various animal forms?" I asked snidely.

Ballsy, I like it, a voice joined in, sounding practically gleeful.

"And who the hell is that?" I growled, glancing around like the ghost girl would suddenly appear.

"My sister," they answered in unison, one echoing in my head as the other echoed in my ears.

"I got that," I replied tersely, scanning the clearing warily. The second I'd shifted back to human form I'd lost the scent of the woman in front of me, a fact I was both grateful for and disturbed by – losing my normally acute sense of smell was practically like amputating a limb but her intoxicating scent was a distraction I didn't need.

"Then why ask?" She snipped back, rolling her eyes – one a deep amber and the other a blue so light it might as well be white. She was distinctive, not beautiful, and I couldn't help but stare. Those mesmerizing eyes cut toward me as she added mockingly, "Let me guess…you've never seen a woman's bare breasts before." I blinked, shaking off my stupor before it got me killed. She sighed, shaking her head and making the messy bob she sported catch the last rays of sun. I swore each strand was a different shade of blonde ranging from the darkest gold to pure white.

"You have the strangest coloring I've ever seen," I blurted out, still caught off guard by her appearance. She seemed to practically glow in the encroaching darkness, a beacon for the weary and lost.

"Way to state the obvious, Captain America," she grunted, dismissing me with a turn of her shoulder.

"Caleb," I introduced quickly, hoping she would give me her name at least. She glanced over her shoulder, but didn't bother to introduce herself.

"I don't want to know your name, *Captain America*." Her eyes never left mine. "*You. Are. Not. Welcome. Here*," she enunciated slowly. Her gaze shifted over my shoulder to the darkening forest. "Exit's that way."

I raised my hand, wanting to stop her, but froze when she flinched, the movement so subtle I shouldn't have been able to detect it, much less react to it. She stared as I lowered my arm awkwardly. "I've been searching for you," I blurted out. "Years. I've wandered all over the country, just looking for something. For you. For this. This place," I rambled, my tongue darting out to wet my lips as those striking eyes held mine. "I can't leave. I don't know when I'll be able to come back," I admitted, knowing the second I returned to Navarre land I'd be stuck there.

She twisted back around and my heart gave a hard thump. She marched up to me, her finger stabbing my chest, those brilliant eyes flashing. "That's the point, Captain America. You ***don't*** come back. Not sure I can make this much clearer for you."

I grabbed her wrist, tightening my grip when she tried to slip from my hold. I didn't let go even as I sensed her panic in the heartbeat that suddenly began to race under my fingertips. "You felt it," I murmured. "There's no way you didn't." I inhaled deeply, my lip curling in frustration at the absence of her scent. "I don't know what this place is, but there was no mistaking that scent," I growled, desperate for her to acknowledge what I'd felt.

She leaned forward, her heart rate slowing as she forcibly controlled her panic, and I couldn't help but feel a surge of admiration. "Forget it. Forget me. Run as far away from here as you can and never come back." She yanked her wrist from my hold, backing away as her eyes warned me it wouldn't be so easy to catch her next time.

I opened my mouth, ready to protest, when her gaze flickered to the side. Her pupils dilated in horror as her lips parted to give a warning. There was no time to react though as I felt my knees crumble, my mouth still open as I landed on hard earth, the sound muffled by a thick layer of leaves. Dread didn't hit until her eyelashes lowered in apology, covering those extraordinary eyes, and I realized her harsh dismissal had been meant to protect me.

Chapter Four

Caleb

He's handsome, a voice commented, the lilting sound drifting through my head and nagging at me with its familiarity.

He's a fool, another answered irritably and *her* voice cleared the fog, reminding me exactly where I was and who was chatting in my head.

So you like him? The other voice prodded teasingly, and I remained silent as I realized they didn't know I was awake. I didn't need to see her to know her face formed an impatient grimace. I still didn't know her name, but I could already anticipate her reactions.

Then that would make me the fool, she responded curtly. *There's no point being interested in a dead man.* The words didn't concern me as much as her tone – a desperate, resigned frustration lacing each one, as if she'd been through this before and already knew the outcome.

Maybe not, the other one said hopefully, telling me she still retained her youthful innocence. *Maybe....maybe he's the one.*

I felt *her* sigh, no doubt biting back a harsh denial. *Gran is expecting us*, was all she finally said and I sensed her warmth moving away from me, but I didn't risk opening my eyes.

I'll be there in a minute, the younger one answered, sounding cagey even to me.

Whatever you're planning, don't, she ordered, sounding more tired than upset. *It's not worth her anger.*

The lightest brush of a finger along my injured leg disrupted my curiosity about who the woman she spoke of was, and reminded me I wasn't at full strength.

I can fix it, the younger argued, her attitude suggesting one born with a stubborn doggedness. *She doesn't know about his leg.*

Then you're the fool if you believe that, she answered harshly, her tone turning implacable with her next words. *And you deserve the punishment she'll give you.*

A door opened and closed, leaving an unexpected void in the room when she left. I almost forgot about the younger one until her hands settled on my leg, her touch highlighting the damage. My eyes flew open and I caught my first glimpse of the elusive sister.

"Not what I expected," I said idly, taking in the stick straight white blonde hair that draped down, covering most of her face as she leaned intently over my damaged leg. She didn't so much as twitch at my statement and my eyes narrowed. She laid her palms gently on either side of my leg and a warm sensation began to pulse through my leg. "What are you doing?" I asked sharply, and again didn't receive a response.

Abruptly, I sat up, knocking her away from my injured leg and she fell back, her eyes wide with shock as she stared up at me. This time I took in a matched pair of ice blue eyes, so light blue they might be considered colorless, framed by equally pale eyelashes. In fact, she was so white she could be the poster girl for this Ghost Pack.

Terror filled her eyes and I felt my chest clench in response. There was something intrinsically innocent about her and I couldn't help but feel protective over her even as I was the one who caused her fear. "I'm not going to hurt you," I promised, but her frightened expression didn't fade. She scrambled backwards in a wild panic and I held my hands out, trying to appear nonthreatening. "I appreciate your help," I nodded to my leg and she hesitated for a brief second. "You're deaf," I guessed, unsurprised when I still didn't get a reaction.

You're deaf, I tried again and this time those eerie eyes shot to mine. *I'm right?* She nodded warily, no longer trying to escape me as her gaze darted back to my leg. *You want to fix it? My leg,* I questioned mentally, wondering where exactly I'd found myself as I telepathically communicated with a non-Pack member. She nodded again, scooting a little closer as she eyed me carefully to see if I was going to pounce. *You think you can fix it?*

Her chin tilted up as she replied, *I know I can.* Her eyes admonished me. *If you don't interrupt me again.* I lifted my hands in the universal gesture of backing away and she reached for my leg again. I fought the need to move as my leg spasmed, knowing she was on the edge of scampering away again. Her fingers trembled as she lightly pressed them against my leg and once again heat curled through my leg.

I stared as the scar that had formed slowly faded until there was no trace of it left and grunted when my bone snapped back into place, fixing the improperly healed break. *What is this?* I asked, awed by her ability.

Healing, she responded simply, shrugging lightly as if it was completely normal. Her forehead wrinkled. *How did you know I was deaf?*

It was my turn to shrug. *You didn't respond when I spoke.* One side of my mouth curled up as I added, *And your coloring. If you were a dog, I would have figured it out sooner.*

How are you talking to me? She questioned, squinting at me suspiciously.

I could ask you the same, I retorted, flexing my foot experimentally and causing her to scuttle across the room. *You started it.*

She shook her head, pale strands of hair glittering under the florescent light above. *I've always been able to project my voice.* My eyebrows raised at her description of her ability. *But you're the first one outside my tribe who has ever answered.*

Is that why you think I'm the one? I questioned, shelving away the fact that she referred to her Pack as a tribe, as her eyes widened.

You were listening to us, she accused, crossing her arms as she attempted to glare at me. It fell short since I'd already been witness to her sister's glare and it far outstripped this little pup.

Kind of hard not to since you were having the conversation in my head, I retorted and her expression turned uncertain. *Honestly, nothing has been close to normal since I crossed onto your Pack's land,* I added, rubbing the back of my neck. *Who hit me and where am I?* My gaze swept the room, noting the bars on the door and ceiling were reinforced steel, purposely designed to keep someone or something with greater than average strength contained.

She darted for the door, suddenly skittish, but I choose to remain still. Not escaping while I had the chance was a risk, but I suddenly found myself reluctant to leave. There was something here…

Who was I kidding?

She had captured my attention and for the first time in a very long time I had zero desire to move on. Letting her little sister slide out the door unscathed, I settled back against the cold stone wall, content to wait until *she* came back for me, not a single doubt in my mind that she would.

Chapter Five

Dru

"You're late, Paige," Gran intoned, also projecting her voice mentally for Paige's sake. Gran's double voice grated against my sensitive hearing, aggravating me more than normal. Paige curtsied, her smile full of apology as she came to a stop in front of the table. She knew there was no point in sitting down until Gran gave her permission. "You know dinner is served precisely at seven o'clock. Your tardiness has forced us to wait. Dare I ask what you thought was more important?"

I stopped by chapel to light a candle for Sister Margaret and lost track of time, Paige answered, her dulcet tones soothing the raw edge of my temper. She'd never once spoken aloud, but I was positive I would be able to recognize her voice in the loudest of rooms. I stared down at the empty plate in front of me, the delicate porcelain china out of place in the rough stone and wood house, and fought a smile. Paige had figured Gran out by the time she was two, and where I had a tendency to butt heads with Gran, Paige somehow always managed to escape her wrath.

It is truly a good thing I adore you, little sister, I told her as Gran harrumphed, but gestured for Paige to sit.

Why? She questioned me privately and I shook my head.

"The prisoner is injured. That should even the odds," Gran announced as she served herself. Paige's eyes rounded in panic and I surreptitiously kicked her ankle.

I assumed a puzzled expression as I turned to Gran. "Injured?" I questioned, accepting the dish she handed me.

"He was wounded by one of the traps," she stated, her fierce hawk eyed stare daring me to contradict her. "The trap had blood all over it."

"From the deer," I answered, careful to keep any hint of argument out of my voice. My gaze flashed to Paige, warning her to play along. "A deer had tripped the trap where we caught the intruder sniffing around."

"I saw no deer," Gran answered, her voice echoing dangerously. She spoke both mentally and aloud, never making an exception for when it was just the three of us, so I was forced to endure her words doubly.

It had escaped, Paige joined in, blinking innocently. *Dru followed the blood trail after you subdued the man.*

"*Drusilla*," Gran barked, causing us to both jump. "Why do you persist with these ridiculous nicknames?" She seethed, distracted from the injured prisoner by one of her most famous pet peeves. "She is not a man. You do not call her *DRU*, you call her by her proper name."

Yes, Gran, Paige bowed her head, by all appearances contrite, but I knew it was mostly to hide her smile. Gran's ice blue eyes burned, but she let it go, turning instead to me.

"Where is it?" She snapped and I played dumb.

"Where is what?"

She exhaled, her mouth pulling down as she lost patience. "Don't play the fool, Drusilla. The *deer*. If it was a deer in the trap, where is the deer?"

It ran off, Paige answered, desperately trying to save me. *Remember, I told you, Dru...silla followed its trail,* she added, quickly correcting herself.

"And Drusilla wouldn't leave a wounded animal to die in the woods. Nor would she allow meat to go to waste when there are hungry bellies to feed," Gran replied, her eyes cold enough to freeze my insides.

I'm sorry! Paige's remorseful apology blasted through my brain as I held Gran's expectant gaze.

Its fine, I replied to Paige, dismissing her apology. We were who we were and not even Gran's constant attempts could change that. Paige was going to heal any wounded creature she came across, Captain America included, and I was going to do whatever it took to protect Paige.

"I brought the deer to Strickland so he could process it and pass the meat to the most needy," I answered Gran and only the tiniest twitch of her eyebrow told me I'd surprised her. Clearly, she hadn't had the chance to talk to Strickland yet, but I knew she would demand a detailed description of the deer carcass. I whispered another apology to the poor deer whose leg I had butchered after killing it, grateful Gran's sense of smell wasn't good enough for her to detect the difference between human and animal blood on the trap itself. I'd cleaned it, but another wolf would be able to tell and could potentially out my lie.

I stared hard at the plate, the faded rose pattern blurring as I considered the punishment she would mete out if she discovered this lie. I wasn't sure even Paige's healing ability would be enough to save me.

"I'll speak with Strickland after dinner," Gran stated, effectively ending the conversation. I picked up my fork, careful not to betray my shakiness, and started to eat.

I'm sorry, Paige cried out to me, showing not a single hint of her internal turmoil as she delicately buttered a roll. *I should have listened to you.*

Her remorse was like a wave crashing over me, threatening to suck me under. I clutched the fork in my hand tightly, letting the emotion flow over me instead of take me. *Easy, Paige*, I chided and the emotional wave disappeared in a flash. *You were going to help him. I just made it so Gran wouldn't know.*

*But if I hadn't....*she trailed off.

But you did. I knew you would.

You're always covering for me, she fussed internally, while outwardly she ate a bite of fish and gave no indication of our mental conversation. *You should let me face the consequences.* I shuddered internally at the thought even as her guilt pushed at me. Paige never could hide her emotions.

I will never allow you to face Gran's consequences, I swore as dinner churned dangerously in my stomach at the idea of Gran ever punishing Paige. I changed the subject, needing her to forget this sudden display of consciousness. *Captain America all better?*

*Yes, I healed his leg, but I need to tell you….*Paige broke off as Gran said her name.

"Paige," Gran interrupted whatever Paige was about to tell me. "If you are going to play with your food, then you are clearly not hungry. You are dismissed." Paige gave me a helpless glance, but stood from the table, laying her napkin precisely over the plate to indicate she was finished. Silence fell over the table until Paige was out of earshot, then Gran declared, "Watch her."

My head jerked toward Gran, startled by her directive. She had never shown any indication that she doubted Paige so my nod was slow in coming. "May I ask why?" I risked, keeping my eyes lowered.

"I don't want the foolish child becoming moon-eyed over a handsome face," Gran replied, her voice clipped, as the air escaped me in a rush, stunned by her answer. "You will deal exclusively with the prisoner. I expect your pragmatic nature will serve you well in this instance."

I dipped my chin in acknowledgement, knowing it was pointless to argue, not that I wanted to this time. Instead of having to finagle a reason to see him, Gran had handed me the perfect excuse. "Of course," I said simply, setting my fork down. "If you'll excuse me, I'll see to hi-," I cut myself off before she could conclude my pragmatic nature had also been swayed by a chiseled jaw. "The prisoner," I corrected hastily.

She inclined her head and I was careful not to rush, wiping my mouth then delicately folding my napkin. "Have a good evening," I offered politely before turning to leave the room. My shoulders didn't relax until I was out of her line of sight and then my strides grew longer.

I needed to set a few things straight with Captain America before he got us killed.

***

My gaze swept the clearing as I approached the cellar, but no one was around. The few who were left tended to keep inside after dark, a lesson Paige said I needed to learn. She could never understand that nothing out here scared me, that the darkness was the only place where I could be myself.

I padded silently down the stone steps, my hand trailing on the damp wall as the pupil in my amber eye dilated, allowing my eyesight to sharpen in the dim light. A pebble caught under my foot, and I winced as it skittered down the steps, announcing my arrival.

He was standing, arms crossed over a muscular chest while a pair of baggy shorts preserved his modesty, when I stopped at the door. "You're awake," I observed, somehow unsurprised he'd managed to shake off Gran's spell so quickly. His left eye twitched and my own narrowed in response. A question bubbled on my lips but he moved, so quickly I flinched, giving me a rare taste of my own medicine.

"You came."

Strong fingers wrapped around the bars as he studied me, bright blue eyes catching mine, and I hurried to lower them before he saw more than I wanted. My gaze fell to his hands, taking note of the calluses as he tightened his grip.

I inhaled, the musky scent of male filling my lungs, and raised my eyes. "We need to talk."

He released the door and spread his arm in welcome. The corner of my mouth curled up in a shadowy smile as I faintly shook my head. "I'll stay here," I commented and he lifted one shoulder.

"Your prerogative." A flash of white accompanied his next words, "I don't bite."

A choked laugh escaped me at the clear lie. I tapped my nose. "I think yours just grew an inch."

"It's not the only thing," he remarked, eyes glinting and I felt my cheeks heat uncomfortably at the innuendo. He smoothed his expression when he saw my discomfort. "You wanted to talk?"

I nodded at his leg. "Paige fixed your leg."

He tilted his head, lifting his hand to mid-chest like a marker. "Blonde? Blue eyed? Skittish little thing?"

My heart caught at his description, then started pounding. I slammed my hands against the bars that now protected him from me as I snarled, "Leave her alone."

He backed away, raising his hands. "I didn't touch her," he swore, his eyes steady on mine. "It's not your little sister I'm interested in."

"You saw her?" I questioned, my voice dangerously low.

He nodded slowly, watching me.

"Explain," I demanded.

"When you two were in here," he indicated the cage with a flick of his fingers, "I woke up as you were talking."

My forehead wrinkled as I said, "But that was hours ago."

His eyes widened questioningly, but I shook my head, waving my hand for him to continue as I processed the new information.

"You left. She healed my leg," he concluded quickly, pacing back toward me. His hands settled on either side of mine, their warmth matching my own. "That's all."

I raised my head to meet his beautifully matched eyes, their color rivaling an October sky. "You spoke to her," I said, letting my voice lift encouragingly on the last word. He squinted, eyeing me suspiciously. "Don't lie," I warned, my fingers curling tightly around the bars as our breath mingled in the cold air.

"Spoke isn't exactly the word I'd use," he replied carefully, his gaze never leaving mine. "Seeing as how she doesn't speak." All the air left me in a rush as my head bumped the bars.

"You know."

"That she's deaf?" He lowered his head, a little too close for comfort but I didn't pull back, trusting the bars to keep him at a distance. "I noticed."

"She talked to you."

He cocked his head. "We had a conversation."

It was my turn to glance at him questioningly, keeping my eyelashes lowered to hide my mismatched eyes.

She seemed surprised when I answered, he answered mentally, testing me and I heard him exhale when I blinked. *You can hear me.* It was a statement but I dipped my head in acknowledgement anyway. *Talk to me*, he pleaded, our faces separated only by the bars of the cage I'd placed him in.

"I thought we had been talking," I replied, continuing to speak aloud.

Not what I mean, he chided and I pressed my lips together, knowing what he wanted. *Please.*

"Why does it matter?" I asked, feeling desperate as the moment grew more intimate. "There's no need for me to speak to you telepathically."

You do it with your sister, he retorted, his lips twisting to form a pout, and I flattened my mouth before a smile could escape.

"Out of necessity," I reminded him, keeping my expression severe.

You could do it with me, he cajoled and I shook my head again.

"Why does it matter?" I repeated.

It's something Pack mates do, he answered.

"Something we're not," I was quick to point out. He ducked his head, and I sucked in a shaky breath at his nearness.

We could be more, he claimed, the thought a gossamer strand linking us. My eyes drifted shut as a fierce pang of longing shot through me. It wasn't often I thought about the things I'd missed out on, but somehow he managed to stir up memories I'd thought long buried.

"That," my tongue darted out, moistening suddenly dry lips, "That would be a mistake."

Would it? He questioned, his voice sounding far away. Warm breath drifted over my forehead. *What's your name?* My eyes popped open at the abrupt subject change and his cheek creased, revealing a dimple. *Come on, you know you want to tell me.*

"Actually, I don't think I do, *Captain America*," I retorted, straightening my spine. "You won't be around long enough to use it." His eyes narrowed the tiniest bit but his next question took me by surprise.

"What's with the Captain America?" He glanced down at himself and I was hard-pressed not to do the same. "Do I look like a solider boy to you?"

"You got the boy part right," I sniped and his lip curled up in amusement. "But it's more the blond, blue-eyed, corn fed look you have going."

"Ahh," he nodded understandingly. "I can see everything but the corn fed bit." He leaned forward confidingly, our foreheads almost brushing. "I'm more a meat eater to be honest." I bit the inside of my lip to keep from smiling and he squinted, angling his head. "Are you? Is that a smile trying to escape?" I shook my head the tiniest bit and he hummed. "Not sure I'm buying it, Princess."

His condescending nickname wiped any hint of a smile from my expression as I glared at him. "What did you call me?"

"Prin-cess," he enunciated helpfully, nodding. "Since you like nicknames I thought I'd give you one."

"And *that's* the one you came up with?" I rolled my eyes, glancing off to the side. "How original."

"Captain America," he stated, wrinkling his nose. "I think we're gonna have to call it even on the originality, *Princess*." His arms snaked through the bars, hanging on either side of me like some sort of twisted embrace. He shrugged, "I mean, if you want to tell me your name…."

"No," I snapped, dropping my hands as I prepared to step away before I did something truly stupid, like tell him. He stirred up feelings, emotions I'd never felt before, and knew better than to act on. His eyes were bright in the dark cell, glinting happily even though he was locked in a cage. I could almost swear he was content to remain here. "I should go," I muttered, backing away when one of his long arms snagged my baggy shirt, stopping me. "*What* are you doing?" I asked snappishly, almost sighing at the attempt to delay me. The thought of being afraid didn't even enter my mind since I knew I could easily get away.

"Making the best mistake of my life," he answered cryptically, his mouth stopping the automatic question about to escape me. My parted lips gave him an advantage as he caught my lower lip between his teeth, sucking lightly. Stunned disbelief held me frozen as I experienced my first kiss at the hands of this intruder, a prisoner whose life would be forfeit if my grandmother knew what he was doing.

A sharp sting had me jerking my head back as blood welled on my lip. "What the hell? What have you *done*?" I hissed, as I gingerly prodded the swollen bite mark. Red smeared the tip of my finger as something slammed into my mind, unstoppable and irrevocable. "What have you done?" I choked, staring at the blood on my hand. I looked up at him then and saw the apology on his face.

I'm sorry. I didn't just *see* his sincerity, I could *feel* it as I stumbled away from him, shaking my head.

You shouldn't have done that, I thought, unable to speak past the fear threatening to choke me. My heart raced frantically, each beat telling me to run.

I'm sorry. It was the only thing I could think of to make you give me a chance.

My eyes flashed to his at that and the way his head jerked back, I knew my single blue eye glowed white. "You should have thought harder," I managed to grit out, the words barely audible but I knew he heard them as his Adam's apple bobbed. I stumbled up the stairs before falling on all fours and crawling the final steps. His regret was a balloon filling my head until I couldn't hear my own thoughts and out of desperation, I shifted.

Bones cracked and tendons shredded as my body twisted in on itself, but the excruciating pain pushed him from my mind as my body knitted itself back together in the form of a slender golden wolf, one blue eye and one amber eye shining in the dark night.

Smells bombarded me instantly, *his* scent overwhelming, and my legs moved before my mind could form a thought, powerful strides taking me down a familiar path as they carried me far away from my mate.

Chapter Six

Caleb

Regret swelled as she disappeared from view, her thoughts an anguished knot that threatened to do me in. A sharp pain distracted me, growing into a burning agony that finally broke the connection my bite had formed between us and I collapsed on the hard ground, panting as it felt like every bone in my body was trying to heal itself from imaginary breaks.

I rolled onto my back as my chest heaved, jerky breaths escaping me. The night sky shined above me between the iron bars of my cage and I stared at them until the pain eased, leaving only a glowing ember in my mind, and I could feel it getting further away as her wolf ran.

I stared at the sky above, guilt flooding me as I contemplated what I'd done. Dom's voice filled my head, the memory of one of his many lessons reprimanding me, "A good leader doesn't force his will on those under his protection. He guides them and gives them the choice." Remorse threatened to choke me as I remembered her face, the horror as she stared at the blood on her finger, and asked me what I'd done.

I rubbed my chest, the weight of a thousand anvils pressing down, as I admitted to myself that I'd forced my will on her. I didn't need to try and imagine Dom's disappointment because it couldn't compare to my own. The memory of her face tormented me and I rolled myself up, yanking off the shorts in one smooth motion before I started the shift. The air shimmered and a sandy colored wolf appeared, bright blue eyes still cloudy from human thoughts.

I shook myself, thick scruff jiggling as I stretched in my new form, my human emotions fading as my other senses took over. *Her* sweet scent hit my sensitive nose and I couldn't help the whimper that escaped. I wanted to crawl on my belly, bare my throat so she would understand how sorry I was for forcing the mating claim without her permission. My paws itched with the need to run, to chase her down, and let our wolves solve the problems our humans had created.

I paced instead.

The cage growing smaller with each turnaround.

Until a strange scent marred the damp air, the smell of gunpowder and ozone mingling and causing my nose to twitch.

She appeared, silent as a ghost and equally terrifying, and it was all I could do not to roll over and show her my belly. My head bowed under the weight of her stare as my fur stood on end. Power, subtle but strong, pulsed from her, crackling in the air between us.

"I should have known," she spoke aloud, vitriol dripping from each word. "Are you here to steal another of my children?" There was no mistaking her question as anything but a dare and my head lowered further as I panted, trying not to fold under the command she wielded. "You won't succeed. That I can promise you." She crouched, her bearing regal, and familiar ice blue eyes examined me, strands of silver hair floating on currents of static electricity, as she sneered, "There is nothing here for you but death, *wolf.*"

I raised my eyes, my lip curling as I bared my teeth, drawing on the long dormant power of an Alpha as I met her gaze, refusing to bend to her will. Her stare sharpened at my show of defiance and her mouth twisted.

"You cannot win," she snarled and her eyes glowed as my front legs buckled, sending me crashing to the ground. She leaned close, only the bars separating us, but I couldn't even snap at her as she hissed, "Don't fear, *wolf.* Your death won't be in vain. I'll hang your carcass from the trees to warn any others who may attempt to cross our borders."

Unwillingly, my eyes closed and I fought as unconsciousness tried to take me, only succumbing when the acrid scent disappeared and I know she was gone.

***

Up....You! Wake....now! Words attempted to penetrate the fog, each one distant and I grasped at them, trying to make order from them. Something nudged my side and I rolled reflexively. *Finally! Wake UP!* The last was a scream and my eyes jerked open to see an angel standing above me, hands on her hips, as she proceeded to kick me with one foot.

"Ow," I grunted, moving out of reach of her sharp strike. *Stop!* I ordered when she went to swing again. *What are you doing?* I asked, recognizing the white haired girl methodically kicking the shit out of me.

Saving your life, she answered, tossing her hair. *I see you met Gran*, she paused, chewing her lip, *again.*

Gran? I questioned, wondering if she could possibly mean the terrifying old lady who'd put me on the ground without lifting a finger. *That's your – grandmother?*

Paige nodded, leaning down to grab the pair of shorts I'd discarded the night before, *Yep. The one and only.* She tossed them on my lap and I reached for them. *You should just go ahead and shift*, she commented, glancing over her shoulder. I hesitated, not remembering shifting back into human form.

Why are you in here? I asked again, seeing the door was wide open and Paige didn't look too concerned. *Aren't you supposed to be guarding me?* I nodded to the open door. *I could escape.*

She gave me a pitying smile. *That's kind of the point, not to state the obvious here.* She tapped her fingers nervously. *You need to hurry. I'm not supposed to be down here.*

Why not? I questioned, getting to my feet as she kept her eyes firmly fixed on the wall. *You were here yesterday.*

That was before Gran decided I might fall for your handsome face, Paige replied nonchalantly as I choked. Her head tilted as she gave me a considering look. *You are good looking, but you're kinda old.*

I'm twenty-eight, I protested, wondering when that had made me old.

She gave a surprised laugh, muttering to herself, *Wait till Dru finds out you're younger than her.*

Dru? I questioned sharply, wondering if I'd finally found the name of my elusive mate. She suddenly became evasive, shaking her head.

You need to go. She made a shooing motion with her hand and I crossed my arms, not budging. *Seriously, Dru told me to come let you out. You're supposed to follow her scent off our lands and then go home.*

Where's your sister? I demanded, reluctant to go anywhere without seeing her. Paige's chest heaved with a long suffering sigh.

She waved at the door. *Making a path. For you.* Her stare tried to make it seem like I was an idiot, but the small hitch in her voice caused my eyes to narrow. *Okay, fine, I don't know exactly where she is, but I'm sure she's fine.* She stared at me impatiently. *Trying to save you,* she reminded me, motioning to the door, growing more nervous as time ticked by.

A scraping sound drew my attention and I glanced up. *Someone's coming,* I muttered idly, but her reaction was anything but as she dashed to the door, drawing it closed gently as I watched. She ran to the corner and squeezed into a niche in the rock I hadn't seen previously. I knew she was there, but the longer I stared the harder it was to see her. My gaze kept skimming the spot where she hid, but I was soon distracted by a large man stomping down the stairs.

His head swung around, and I held my breath as his gaze went right over where Paige hid, exhaling as he squinted at me. "Thought I heard talking," he barked, his squint daring me to deny it.

"I got lonely," I said, spreading my hands. "When I get lonely, I talk to myself." He scoffed at my admission but still I stuck my hand through the bars. "Caleb Bradshaw, member of the Navarre Pack." He sneered at the sight of my hand and I curled my fingers into my palm. "Take it you're not a fan."

"You're not welcome here," he grunted and my eyebrows lifted.

"You don't say."

"If was up to me, I'd lock you up and throw away the key," he added and I shook my head as he stared at me through the bars. His nose wrinkled as he sniffed the air. "You smell that?"

I didn't smell a thing but I wasn't about to admit that to this meathead. "Well, I wasn't going to say anything, but yes." He grunted, as Paige yelped, *What are you doing?* I ignored her as I went right up to the bars. I motioned for him to come closer and he lumbered forward. "Just between us," I said confidingly, "You reek. Like a dead rat locked in a box for a month under a hot summer sky." He growled, his fist flying much faster than I would have anticipated for such a beefy guy and striking me right through the bars. I reeled back, laughing as I spat blood on the ground. "What? Can't take a joke?"

A glob of spit landed at my feet as he muttered, "I'll be glad to watch you die."

"You and everyone else," I commented. "Sounds like you need a new source of entertainment around here."

You might be the stupidest man I've ever met, Paige spoke up, sounding impressively awed. *Strickland is my grandmother's right hand man.*

Now you tell me, I groaned as he waddled up the stairs. *You don't think you could have mentioned that sooner?*

I didn't know you were going to poke the bear! Paige popped up in front of the bars, startling me. She swung the door open and this time I exited. *Finally,* she sighed in relief. *I actually like you.*

I paused. *What do you do with the ones you don't like?* She pressed her lips together, pretending she hadn't heard and I shook my head. *The pair of you worry me.*

Just go home, she pleaded, her gaze darting around the room. *Things will go back to normal when you do.* I wasn't sure what to make of her idea of normal but I definitely wasn't going home. I wasn't sure where home was anymore. The only thing I was sure of was one little she wolf.

I'm going to find your sister, I replied and Paige's face fell.

I don't think that's a good idea, she protested hastily and my smile turned wolfish.

The best ones never are, I replied with a wink, leaping up the stairs as I left her there, a puzzled expression on her face.

A deep breath at the top of the stairs told me zilch so I dropped the shorts I was holding and shifted, raising my nose as I inhaled, the first rays of sunlight peeking through the trees. Her trail was impossible to miss and I let my wolf take the lead, stretching our legs after the confinement of the cell.

I weaved through the forest, pausing periodically to see if there were any other scents, but strangely hers was the only one. I followed her trail until I came to a fork. Her scent went both ways, with the fresher trail going left and I suspected that was the one I was meant to take.

I eyed it, knowing it was the smarter choice. There was something going on here that I didn't understand and staying might cost me my life. Dru had made it clear she wanted me gone and at the moment I couldn't blame her.

My head swung right and I trotted forward, my nose to the ground to pick up the weak scent trail. After a while, I could see where a faint path had formed and my strides lengthened, instinct driving me forward.

The forest ended abruptly, golden light almost blinding me after the dim woods. She sat cross legged on a large flat rock, looking out over a deep valley, her hair shining in the morning sun. She shook her head, calling over her shoulder, "How did I know you'd take the wrong path?"

I shifted, walking forward to find a pair of loose sweatpants folded neatly on the ground. I quickly dragged them on, scratching my belly as I studied her.

She was more relaxed than I'd seen her and I had a feeling she came here often. "I took the one less traveled by, and that has made all the difference," I quoted and a chuckle escaped her.

"Frost."

"You know your poets," I commented.

"I know that one line," she corrected. "And only because my father read it to me as a child."

"I met your grandmother," I mentioned and her eyes closed as she shook her head ruefully.

"And yet, you still followed me."

"I admit, she didn't seem to like me, but I feel like I could get her to warm up to me eventually." A choking sound filled the air and I stepped forward in concern, but then a peal of laughter rang over the valley and I realized she was laughing at me. I stopped, stunned by the sight of her smile and the fact that I had put it there.

"You truly are a fool," she cried in the midst of her laughter. "Trust fate to give me an insane mate."

"I prefer confident," I retorted, padding forward as her head swung toward me. "I can be very charming. Some even say diplomatic." She propped her head on her palm, her hair swinging forward to cover her blue eye, and I took a chance, hopping up to sit next to her. "You're not going to push me off, are you?" I cast a wary glance down, just now noticing the sheer drop off.

"I guess that's a chance you'll have to take," she replied, wiggling over to give me more room. "It would solve a problem," she added contemplatively, eyeing me. "Since you seem reluctant to leave."

"What can I say? The hospitality is hard to resist and the people are so welcoming." She snorted and I waved my arm. "Can't get views like this where I'm from either."

"And where's that?" Her question surprised me but when I glanced over she was studiously avoiding my gaze.

"South, directly south. Our pack lands border yours to the south."

"You're a Hanley?" She sneered in disbelief, both those mismatched eyes pinning me. I hurriedly shook my head.

"No, no. I'm from the Navarre Pack. The Hanleys were defeated and my Alpha took over. Dominic Navarre." She still gazed at me suspiciously so I kept talking. "I swear it's true." I looked over the sun kissed valley, calculating rapidly. "I mean, it's been ten years now since the Hanley Alpha was killed." I glanced back at her. "You haven't had any trouble with them have you?"

She yanked her gaze away, not answering, but her fingers trembled.

"Dru," I said quietly, grateful Paige had let her name slip.

Her lips twisted. "And here I was starting to warm up to Princess." I grinned, scooting a tad closer and her eyes cut toward me. "That wasn't an invitation, Cap'n."

"Caleb," I repeated, knowing she hadn't forgotten but trying to see if she'd use it.

"I'm not senile, thank you very much."

"I didn't think you were," I rushed to reassure her and she plucked at the hem of her jeans. "I'm just eager to hear my name on your lips."

"That is a terrible pickup line."

"It's not a line," I protested, laying back on the rock. She hunched forward, not seeming concerned that her back was exposed. "We're mates."

"Thanks to you," she snarled, gesturing to her lip. "It's puffy."

"In all fairness, you started it," I pointed out gently and she twisted, staring at me in disbelief. I shaded my eyes, trying to decide if she really didn't know. "You bit me first."

"No, I didn't!"

I cocked my head, wondering how she didn't know. "You did. When you lunged at me."

"I didn't break skin," she contended and I sat up on my forearms as she turned toward me.

"You don't have to break skin," I explained. "You just have to have intent."

"I didn't intend to take you as a *mate*," she snapped, crossing her arms as she glared at me mutinously. "You read it wrong." That startled a laugh out of me that quickly faded when I realized she was serious.

"I didn't read anything into it. You claimed my wolf as your own. I just finished it so we'd have a chance." I opened the gateway in my mind, the path that lead straight to her and only her, the one she'd created, albeit unintentionally I was discovering.

She flinched, her eyelashes lowering as she read the truth in what I was saying and my genuineness. "I didn't know," she admitted hesitantly. She paused for a long moment before asking, "Why did you apologize if it was my fault?"

"You may have started it, but I stole a kiss and a bite without permission," I swallowed, gazing out over the valley so I wouldn't have to meet her piercing stare. "I've had my will taken from me. My choice. I promised I would never do it to another and I did it to *you*." Disgust coated my tongue as I considered that I'd broken my vow with the one person I never wished to harm.

A warm touch distracted me and I glanced down to see she'd rested her pinkie next to my hand. It was the barest of touches, but a sense of comfort washed through me. "You didn't take my will," she finally said. "Not if I was the one who initiated it."

I blinked, giving her a sideways glance. "You didn't know."

"That's not an excuse," she retorted without heat, her eyes set somewhere in the distance. "Not for us. Some part of me understood what I was doing." She took a deep breath and her finger eased away from mine. "Why did you finish it?"

My hand drifted, settling over hers and she glanced at me uncertainly. "Because for the first time in my life, I wanted a reason to stay."

Bitterly, she smiled. "But you can't stay, Caleb." Something settled into place as she said my name, a determination to make this thing work, no matter the consequences. "Not here. Gran will never allow it."

"Then come with me," I countered, lifting our joined hands. "The Navarre Pack will accept you. Welcome you with open arms." She opened her mouth and I hurried to convince her, already seeing the denial in her eyes. "You won't be the only female wolf anymore. We have several. One is an Alpha." Surprise kept her mute so I continued. "Leaving your Pack is hard. I know that. But you'll have me and I promise to help you adapt. You'll have all the time you need to integrate into the Pack."

"Caleb," she said and afraid she was about to say no, I spoke again.

"Dru, consider it at least. Please."

The tiniest smile graced her lips and my heart jumped. "Are you begging?" She questioned with a lift of her eyebrow.

"Yes, if that's what it takes," I answered instantly.

She ducked her head, her hand curling under mine. "What you're saying sounds....amazing."

"Then come," I interrupted, suddenly eager to take her to Navarre land and introduce her to Dom, Jess, Anna, and Trent. "We can go now."

She glanced up at me apologetically. "I won't leave Paige."

"She can come with us," I offered, seeing an easy solution. "No one will care about her differences."

She must have felt the truth in my words because her expression eased and she smiled gently.

"I wish it was that simple."

"We can make it as simple as it needs to be."

"There's so much you don't know," she replied, worrying her lower lip.

"Then explain it to me and we'll figure it out together."

"Paige can't leave and neither can I," she stated, shaking her head resolutely. I saw the determination in her eyes, but it was no match for my own.

"Then we stay."

"I stay," she specified. "You go."

I shook my head, equally determined. "No."

"She'll kill you," Dru reminded me, her voice catching.

"I am particularly hard to kill," I responded, unconsciously tracing the scar on my chest. Her gaze followed the path of my scar, her forehead wrinkling with worry.

"She won't fight you with tooth and claw," Dru warned. "You don't know what you're dealing with here."

"I have you," I answered, bringing my hand up to her face and letting it hover there until she bowed her head in permission. I gently touched the skin under her blue eye, noticing how she kept hiding it from my view. "Together, we can make this work. I know it."

Chapter Seven

Dru

It took every ounce of control I had not to duck my head and hide the eyes I despised from his clear gaze. How he could look at me with such awe, I didn't understand. I was a freak, my differences obvious for the world to see, and he was….perfect.

A fact my grandmother would never see, and she would tear him limb from limb out of fearful ignorance - a reality I could never allow to happen.

"You have to go," I pleaded, terror filling me and I saw when it hit him. I didn't know how to control the connection between us as my emotions spilled over onto him, and I suddenly felt a surge of sympathy for Paige. "I won't allow her to destroy you."

"Neither will I," he promised, his ignorance making him confident of an outcome he couldn't possibly achieve. "I won't allow her to destroy you either."

"She won't. I'm her grandchild," I answered quickly, hoping that would be enough. He smiled, a blend of pity and understanding lacing it.

"She is though." I shook my head, not comprehending, and he explained, "She despises the wolf. She hates half of you." He touched my brow above my amber eye. "I heard it in her voice when she spoke to me. Maybe she doesn't do it intentionally, but she's destroying part of you every single day."

"She doesn't hate me," I denied automatically, not completely believing my own words. "She has her reasons," I finished lamely. He stared at me doubtfully and I rubbed my neck awkwardly. "She won't kill me at least. You, on the other hand…."

"Could die a thousand deaths and she'd smile every time," he concluded and I nodded reluctantly. Gran had no love for wolf shifters, not after everything they'd cost her, and I knew if she could, she'd strip the wolf from me as well. "How could she hate someone she doesn't know?" He shook his head. "I mean no harm."

"And I believe you, but your definition of harm and hers are two very different things," I said as I bent down, missing his curious expression.

"She said something about stealing her children," Caleb declared, his voice lifting in question and I kept my head down as I schooled my expression, but it didn't matter since my shoulders tensed automatically at the mention of my parents. I had the feeling he noticed, but he had the grace not to mention it.

"No idea," I lied easily, straightening up. "You really should go," I suggested once again, not really believing this would be the time he listened, but when his expression turned inward, regret surged through me.

"I really should," he agreed, and I fought the desperate urge to take my words back. Leaving was what was best for him, even though I was starting to realize it wasn't what I actually wanted. It seemed my brain and heart no longer agreed on what was best for me. "But I've never really been good at doing what I should do," he continued and my attention jerked back to him as he grinned wryly. "Something Dom seems to think I should work on."

Happiness crackled through me, but I managed to keep my voice calm as I asked, "Dom?"

"My Alpha," he answered, and I felt his mix of emotions when he said the title.

"You love him," I observed and his eyes snapped to mine in surprise. "I can feel it when you speak of him. So many emotions warring for attention. Only someone you love would cause that."

He dipped his head, his own smile regretful. "It took me too long to realize that." His gaze drifted west, in the direction of his own Pack lands, and I stuffed my hands in my pockets before I did something foolish like reach for his hand. "My relationship with Dom has always been," he paused, taking a deep breath as he searched for the right word, "Complicated."

"Aren't they all?" I muttered under my breath as I considered the two people in my life that mattered most. My relationship with each of them couldn't be more different, but I'd classify them both as *complicated*.

"My entire life he's the one I looked up to, the one whose approval I sought," he cleared his throat, casting his gaze down. "I've disappointed him time and again, but he's never...he's never given up on me." He sighed then let out a chuckle. "And this conversation went somewhere I didn't plan."

"I don't mind," I replied softly, scuffing the ground with my foot, my toes curling in the loose soil. "It's nice to hear about your Pack."

Caleb glanced around curiously. "Is your Pack patrolling? I didn't notice any scent but yours on the trail." I leaned back, resisting the urge to fidget as I tried to come up with an explanation he would believe. His sharp gaze caught my movement as he added casually, "In fact, I haven't noticed any wolves."

Alarm blasted through me, but it wasn't my own. "Paige," I gasped as her emotions slammed into me. Instantly, I was moving, my feet pounding the ground as I raced into the forest. Caleb kept pace, confusion marring his expression as he gamely followed me without understanding.

She knows, Paige's panicked voice broke through the distress and I knew Caleb heard her too when he replied.

Knows what?

He's still here? Paige questioned, sounding hopeful.

What does she know, Paige? I asked, striving for calm as I slowed my reckless pace now that I knew she wasn't in imminent danger. Caleb followed my lead, jogging next to me as we waited for her answer.

That Caleb escaped, she answered quickly, then hesitated.

"Why do I feel like there's more?" Caleb muttered aloud and I glanced at him, silently agreeing. *Paige, she was going to find out I escaped,* he told her patiently. *You let me out,* he reminded her.

My stomach churned as she remained silent, her emotions suspiciously absent. *Paige?*

She thinks you helped him escape, Paige admitted in a rush, the words practically blurring together and I stumbled to a stop as an icy dread trickled through me. Caleb caught my arm, but I'd gone numb as Paige added desperately, *You can't come back. She's furious.*

Fear paralyzed me as I imagined the punishment she would inflict for a transgression this great. Previous punishments drifted through my mind - weeks of being chained so tightly I couldn't shift, being beaten with a cane over and over again until I was forced to shift to heal and then the punishment starting all over, being starved to the point that I couldn't shift.

"Dru," Caleb's voice sounded far away as I wondered if this would be the time she killed me for my disobedience. "Dru, hit me." His command pierced the fog and I blinked at him, sure I'd misunderstood. He nodded, gesturing to his face. "Knock me on my ass."

I gave him a doubtful stare. "It won't work," I murmured, already shaking my head. "She'll know." I swallowed hard, frustrated by the newly discovered inability to hide my emotions from him. I knew he could feel the rush of anxiety as I thought of facing Gran, of dragging him before her and praying she didn't kill us outright.

"Dru, trust me," he stated, rubbing my arms. "Together we can do anything."

Dru? Paige's uncertain voice broke the moment, and stiffened my resolve.

"We have to make it look good."

He nodded, pride creasing his face. "Consider me your punching bag."

Paige, we're coming back.

What? Paige squeaked. *Do you think that's a good idea?*

Not at all, I sighed, my gaze going to Caleb. *But I don't see another option.*

You could leave with him, Paige suggested, striving to be brave, but we both heard the quaver in her voice. *I'll be fine.*

Caleb's jaw firmed in determination and warmth filled me at his protectiveness over my sister. *We're coming back*, he said decisively. *Right after your sister knocks me out.*

Good luck? Paige said uncertainly. *And hurry.*

"No pressure," I muttered, clenching my hands into fists, then shaking them out. "I got this."

"Put the whammy on me," Caleb said and I blinked, distracted from my mutterings.

"Whammy?"

He nodded. "Yeah, that thing where I can't move, like in the forest."

My gaze shifted to the side. "I....can't," I admitted, yet another of my shortcomings brought to his attention. "I don't, I don't have my grandmother's ability."

"She's the one that knocked me out the first day," he stated slowly and I nodded. "You're telling me I got knocked on my ass by an old lady." My lips twitched at his disgust. "I mean I know she's powerful, but…." I pressed my lips together to hide my desire to laugh. "Well, shit." He scratched his head. "Don't tell Dom," he informed me. "Or Trent." I shook my head, not knowing who Trent was or when I'd ever have the opportunity to tell him, but willing to agree since Caleb looked rattled. "Alright, then." He jutted his chin out. "Whenever you're ready."

I balled my fist, ready to swing, but losing my nerve at the last second. "I don't think I can," I confessed, feeling stupid. "You haven't done anything." My shoulders lifted. "You're trying to help my sister."

"You tried to rip my throat out the first time we met," he grunted, staring at me in disbelief. "Now, you're trying to tell me you're a pacifist."

"Not a pacifist," I denied, pointing at him. "But I need a reason."

"You didn't have a reason when I showed up!"

"You were trespassing," I countered. "And we gave you plenty of warning. You just ignored them." I shook my head. "I can't help your poor decision making." One corner of his mouth lifted as he stared at me. "What?" I asked defensively. "It's true."

"But now you can't hit me even though I'm trying to escape."

"Don't turn this around on me," I exclaimed.

He rolled his shoulders. "I'm just saying you won't hit me even though it means protecting your sister…..I guess you don't love her as much as you claim."

My eyes felt like they were going to pop out of my head as my hand clenched and I got in his face. "Do *not* bring Paige into this."

"Seems to me that she's the whole reason for this," he retorted, not backing down as he stepped into my space. "The least you could do is punch me."

I swung without thinking, his head snapping back as a cracking sound filled the air.

He shook it off, smirking as he said, "I think your grandmother hits harder."

Blind rage filled me and I hit him again, this time letting my wolf power it. He flew back, slamming into a tree, and a bloody smile creased his face. "That's my girl."

"I," uppercut, "Am," punch, "NOT," gut punch, "a," my leg swept his feet out from underneath him, "*Girl*," I sneered, panting as I stood over his prone body. He groaned, rolling onto his back. I crossed my arms. "I am a woman."

"But you agree you're mine," he remarked, grinning as he stared up at me. I rolled my eyes, slamming my foot into his head and knocking him out.

"I agree to nothing," I told his unconscious form as I lifted him onto my shoulder with a grunt. "I'm also tired of hauling your heavy ass around."

***

She met me at the edge of the forest, her eyes glowing as she took in his battered face. "This is a dangerous game you play, Drusilla."

"Game?" I dropped him at her feet. "I thought I was doing your bidding."

"Do not mouth off to me," she hissed, stepping forward and I flinched back. "He knows our secret."

"He knows nothing."

"He's seen you."

"As a woman," I lied carefully. "He's curious. Nothing more."

"And when he figures it out?" She demanded. "When his curiosity is satisfied and he exploits you?" My lashes lowered, hiding my eyes from her burning gaze. "When he sells you to the highest bidder?"

"He's not a hunter," I protested, realizing my mistake a second too late.

"And you know this? You would stake your life on it? Your sister's life? The lives of everyone here?" Pressure built with each question, making it hard to breathe, as I waited for the final blow. "Wasn't your father's life enough?"

I bowed my head, my throat tight, as I struggled against the old guilt. I finally managed to reply bitterly, "I'm not a child and he's a wolf, not a hunter."

"And I trust no one," she answered sharply, and I knew she meant absolutely no one, myself included. "Wolf or not, he will destroy us if given the chance. A lesson you should be well versed in, Drusilla."

"I'm a wolf," I reminded her, my stare defiant.

She gripped my chin, her fingers pinching painfully. "You are of *my* blood. You might be a half breed *mutant*, but my blood flows through your veins and I will be damned if I lose another child to a *beast*," she hissed. She forced my head up, intentionally avoiding my amber eye when she met my gaze. "They are not our equals. You would do well to remember that." She released me and I stumbled back. "Put him back and this time make sure he can't escape or I *will* hold you responsible." Fear sent a shiver down my spine at the implied threat, the reaction ingrained, as she swept away, trusting I would do exactly as she commanded.

I grasped Caleb's arms, dragging him toward the underground cell, wishing he'd left when he had the chance, because I knew Gran would never change her mind and without a miracle, he'd die there.

Chapter Eight

Caleb

I kept my body loose as Dru dragged me over the rough ground, not wanting to alert her to the fact that I'd regained consciousness during the conversation with her grandmother. What I'd heard disturbed me, but it was Dru's sense of hopelessness that concerned me the most. Her emotions had been all over the place, and not a single one had been positive, making me even more determined to get her away from her grandmother's influence.

She stopped, and as damp air touched my skin I knew we'd reached the stairs to my cell. I prepared myself for the jarring descent down the steps as she readjusted her grip, but the expected jostling didn't happen. Instead, my body hovered a couple inches above the ground and I floated down the steps next to her.

Suddenly, their mention of a secret took on new meaning. Paige's healing ability could be attributed to wolf genes but I'd never heard of a wolf being able to levitate someone. The door clanged open and I was gently lowered to the cold ground.

Do you want me to heal him? Paige's voice drifted through my mind, even though I knew she'd meant the question for Dru. It appeared I was tuned in to their frequency, a fact they seemed unaware of.

No, it would defeat the purpose of me beating the crap out of him, Dru grumbled and I sensed she stood in the doorway, watching me. *Gran is never going to let him go.*

Maybe she just needs time, Paige suggested hopefully. *She might change her mind when she sees he isn't a threat.*

You didn't hear her. She's made up her mind. She'll only be satisfied when the wolf is gone. My heart thumped painfully at the sadness in her voice, feeling like I was missing something. *She'll do what she always does.* I wanted to shout, "What does she do?" but was afraid if they knew I could hear them they'd clam up. *She'll experiment until there's nothing left of him.* Paige was silent, telling me she didn't have an argument, and I didn't feel any better knowing their grandmother experimented on wolf shifters.

The door scraped as it swung shut, but Dru didn't leave. "Are you awake?"

I debated pretending to still be unconscious but if I'd learned anything in my twenty eight years it was that when someone asked, they already knew. I sat up, wincing as my body protested the movement. "I'm awake," I answered with a groan. "Did you have to bruise the face?" I gingerly prodded my cheek. "All I have are my good looks."

She snorted, a smile fighting to break through and I wanted to pump my arm in victory, except I didn't think my ribs would appreciate it. "If all you had were your good looks, then you're welcome," she teased, her expression lightening.

I grabbed my chest. "Ow, shot right to the heart."

"Your pride, you mean." I scooted back, resting against the wall as she leaned on the bars. "Go ahead," she sighed. "I know you must have heard something."

"More like everything," I admitted and her eyes closed briefly. "We really need to work on your kick." An unwilling chuckle escaped her as her eyes met mine, and once again I was caught by her clear gaze. Her eyes intrigued me. They were a glimpse into the two halves of her soul. I recognized the wolf who stared boldly back at me, but it was the shadows hiding in the cool blue that kept me searching for answers.

"No questions?" She spoke lightly, but her lashes lowered, breaking the connection as our eyes held a beat longer than comfortable.

"Where are the other wolves?" It wasn't the question I meant to ask, and based on her face she wished I hadn't. She pressed her lips together so tightly their soft pink faded to white and I pushed myself up until I was standing. "I haven't seen any, there's no scent but yours, and I haven't heard a single howl."

Her chin tilted up. "Then it sounds like you already know the answer."

"Tell me," I commanded, needing to be sure. "Tell me the truth."

A brittle smile formed as she rocked against the bars. "The truth?" She shook her head. "Wouldn't that be nice?"

"Dru," I said softly and she nodded faintly.

"The truth is I'm the lone wolf here."

I'd suspected something like that but hearing her say the words was a punch to the gut. I opened my mouth to speak, but the words didn't come. I cleared my throat. "How long?" The only lone wolf I'd met was Trent and even he'd had Dom. What Dru was telling me seemed impossible, but it explained so much.

"How long?" She repeated, shrugging lightly. "What do you mean?"

"There were other wolves…right?" I asked, glancing around the cage I was in. "Clearly, there were other wolves. This was built to contain a wolf. What happened to them?"

She gazed at the reinforced steel bars, but her thoughts appeared far away. "They died."

"All of them?" I questioned sharply, moving closer as her emotions pulsed through our link, guilt being the predominant feeling. "Dru," I barked, and her gaze snapped to mine. "I need you to explain. What happened to your father?"

"He was killed by hunters."

My forehead wrinkled, perplexed at how hunters would have gotten the jump on a shifter. "Was there a Pack here then?"

"We had always been a small Pack," Dru replied, her voice faraway. "Gran's husband was the Alpha, my great grandfather."

"Whoa, wait a damn minute," I burst out. "You're telling me your grandmother," I paused, correcting myself, "Great grandmother. The one who is crazy powerful and hates shifters was married to a wolf shifter?"

Dru nodded, watching me warily. I shook my head in disbelief, but motioned for her to continue.

"None of his children or grandchildren could shift." She cast her eyes down. "They all had blue eyes." I nodded but didn't interrupt. "He saw it as a weakness. He blamed Gran." Her gaze lifted to mine, the blue eye glowing faintly. "He tried to cast her aside."

"I take it that didn't go well."

She shook her head lightly. "She took his position."

"I didn't think that was even possible," I muttered incredulously.

"You've felt her power." Dru raised her eyebrow. "Do you doubt her?"

I exhaled. "No."

"The Pack was small but strong under her leadership. We kept to ourselves, but guarded our borders fiercely." The words sounded as if they'd been recited many times when her tone changed. "It wasn't until," she paused, taking a deep breath. "Until I was born that things changed." My hands curled around hers over the bars that separated us. "There had never been one like me."

"Unique, distinctive, one of a kind," I offered, resting my head next to hers. She turned her head so I could only see her amber eye.

"An omen," she said softly. "Harbinger." She swallowed, licking her lips. "My father sensed the wolf inside me, but it was my mother's blood that cursed me," she continued bitterly. I squeezed her fingers gently, wishing I could do more to ease the pain she carried inside. "Some called for my death. They claimed I was unnatural. An abomination." She fell silent, staring at our linked hands. "They may have been right."

"They weren't," I denied instantly, tightening my grip.

She smiled, but there was no happiness in it. "It divided the Pack. Gran gave them a choice. Leave or die." I nodded, for once in complete agreement with her Gran. "A few left." She looked up at me, her eyes shimmering. "It was a mistake. She should have killed them." Anger contorted her face. "They were no longer under oath. They had no loyalty to the Pack. Sparing their lives was not enough to keep them silent."

"The Hanleys attacked us," she murmured. "They thought we were weak. They weren't prepared for Gran. Or my grandmother and mother. Three generations of powerful women." She smiled grimly. "I can only imagine the chaos they unleashed on them. They drove the Hanleys away, but," she paused, her jaw locking. "They managed to kill my grandmother."

"The Hanleys," I verified and she nodded.

"They tore her apart."

I closed my eyes, picturing the horrific scene and starting to understand Gran's hatred for wolves. During my travels, I'd been forced to watch a Pack kill a traitor in their midst and they'd ripped him limb from limb. It wasn't an easy death and for a mother to witness it....Gran's rage was starting to make sense.

"The wolves that stayed were older. Slowly, they all died. Various fights with other wolves who came thinking they could take the Pack and the land. My father was the youngest and he died when I was nine." Remorse flooded through me, but it belonged to Dru.

"What happened to your dad?"

She tucked her head down, and the feeling of guilt increased. "As rumors spread about me, others came looking."

"Others," I repeated.

One of her shoulders tilted up. "Hunters, I'd guess you'd say, but they didn't come looking for a trophy to mount on their wall." Tales I'd heard over the years came back to me, stories of how some hunters captured shifters and sold them to the highest bidder. "I'd never met an outsider." She smiled mockingly. "It's not much of a defense."

"You were...nine?" I commented, thinking back to when she said her father had died. "You can't be held responsible."

"Can't I?" She inhaled, holding her breath for a long second. "I lead them straight to my father. They killed him....so quickly. One breath he was there and then he wasn't." A long exhale. "I had never shifted before and I didn't then. I ran screaming for my mother."

I waited, barely breathing as her eyes lifted to mine, brilliant blue and golden amber fierce in the dim light.

"You think my Gran is terrifying," she whispered softly. "That day I watched my mother flay the flesh from their bones with nothing more than her raging grief." She blinked, washing away any hint of tears. "She saved me, but I will never forget the look on her face when she realized it was at the expense of my father's life. I had broken the rules and brought strangers into our home. A sin so great she would never forgive me."

"You were a child."

"I was the *reason* they were there," she countered bitterly, her voice a barely intelligible snarl. "I cost my father his life. The only person who loved me, who didn't look at me….," she swallowed hard, "Paige never got a chance to know him or our mother because of my actions."

"What happened to your mom?" I forced the question out, not wanting to know, but knowing she needed to tell me.

"Her grief was too much for her." Dru tugged on her lower lip with her teeth. "At least that's how Gran put it, but don't ever ask her about it. Losing a daughter was too much, but a granddaughter as well and over a *wolf?*" I smelled the blood before I saw it as Dru released her lip, the spot where I'd bitten her bleeding again. "She watched me every day waiting for the moment I would shift." She rested her head on the bars, her gaze searching mine. "She tried to stop it, you know. That's why there are so many traps," she whispered the words as if she was telling me a secret. "Unwary wolf shifters, curiosity seekers, or just foolish boys. She thought if she could reverse it, she could stop it."

I had to clear my throat before I could speak. "It didn't work."

Dru's gaze swept the dark, cold pen I stood in. "No, but she learned a lot."

My spine tingled at the hollow words and the memory of bones twisting and breaking, an echo of Dru's pain when she shifted, I suspected. "Your mother died right after your father?"

"My mother committed suicide," Dru corrected me. "It was almost a relief." I jolted at her words and she smiled bitterly. "The way she looked at me? If I'd known how I would have killed myself to escape it."

"Dru." Her name escaped my lips, but I didn't know what to say.

"Two weeks. She *tried*....for two weeks." Bitterness laced her voice. "It's inherited you know." She tapped her blue eye. "Passed down from generation to generation, each one stronger than the last." I reached for her hand as she dug her finger a little too deeply in her eye. "Except when you commit suicide." She smiled at our entwined fingers, knowing what I was doing. "Interesting fact, it goes back to the earth. But her," Dru sighed, "But her grief corrupted it. It's why your senses don't work in human form. It's why there's barely any life in the forest here. Even the animals run from her pain."

I nodded slowly. Her story explained the wrongness I'd sensed in the forest, but it had happened years ago. "It's been twenty years?" I guessed, since Dru had to be at least my age.

"Twenty-one."

"Wouldn't it have faded by now?"

Her mouth quirked. "Our mother had inherited her mother's pain when she died. My mother was powerful indeed."

I didn't know what to make of her answer. For every question Dru had answered, I'd thought of a dozen more, but only one concerned me at the moment. "Why tell me all of this? Why now?"

Dru studied me, then leaned forward until our cheeks touched. "I thought you should know the truth," she whispered softly, brushing her lips against mine before untangling our hands and stepping back. "Before she kills you."

***

Her words lingered long after she had escaped up the stairs. My brain felt overloaded and empty at the same time, and I knew it must have something to do with the mating bond, but at the moment there was no one to ask. My Pack was a scant two hours to the south but it could have been a million miles. I wouldn't drag Dom into a situation I'd created for myself, not at the risk of his life.

And I knew it would be his life at risk.

Dru had given up hope, but I was determined to figure a way out for both of us - no matter how impossible it seemed at the moment.

I paced the cell, not bothering to test the strength of the bars. It wouldn't be brute strength that won this battle. I still wasn't entirely sure what I was up against, other than an old woman powerful enough to oust an Alpha and retain control of his Pack.

"Pack," I whispered to myself. "Ghost Pack, but there is no Pack." I'd aptly named the Pack, albeit unknowingly. It truly was a pack of ghosts. All the wolf shifters were gone or dead besides Dru and it didn't appear like she was under the control of an Alpha.

I stopped pacing, but couldn't remain still, positive I was onto something.

"No Alpha," I muttered aloud, trying to remember long ago lessons from my own Alpha father. He'd drilled them into me repeatedly, trying to shape me into his image, and I'd spent the last decade doing my best to forget them. But now, they might come in handy. "The Pack ceased to exist before Dru shifted, leaving her without a Pack to shift into. Her Gran inherited the previous Pack, but once it was gone, she was no longer Alpha." Technically, everything I was saying was true, but I'd never once heard of a non-wolf shifter being able to assume an Alpha role either. I also still didn't know what Dru's great grandmother *was* exactly, besides insanely powerful.

"And dangerous. Don't forget dangerous," I muttered to myself.

Your lips are moving but there's no one here who can hear you. I twisted to find Paige staring at me, her head tilted curiously. *Dru did beat you up,* she added, sounding impressed.

What are you doing down here? I glanced at the stairs, sure I would have seen her. *How did you get down here?*

I walked? She suggested, giving me a look like she thought I was the crazy one. *How else would I do it?*

I threw up my hands. *Walk through the wall?* At this point, I wouldn't put anything past these blue-eyed women. *What are you?*

How hard did she hit you? Paige asked in concern. *You might have a concussion.*

You are as irritating to talk to as Monster, I muttered and Paige hurried to open the cell door and come inside.

I should heal you. Dru must not have realized how badly injured you were. Paige reached for my head and I moved out of range.

I'm fine, I growled. *Just bruised.*

You're talking about monsters, she exclaimed. *Clearly, you're not fine.*

I blinked at her, then chuckled. *That's his name,* I explained.

You know someone named Monster? She asked in disbelief and I nodded. *Who would name their child that?*

His sister and it's actually very appropriate, I replied, remembering Dom's many stories about Monster's exploits. He'd just turned sixteen and only the combined efforts of Dom and Jess kept him under control. He was too smart for his own good and one of the most powerful wolf shifters any of us had ever seen. Add in the fact that his best friend was also a dominant wolf shifter with Down syndrome who could also ignore his Alpha's orders and Dom had a lot on his hands.

Is the weird name a wolfy thing? She questioned, her hand smacking against my cheek as she surprised me with her speed. *Ha,* she puffed, grinning hugely. *Gotcha.*

I arched an eyebrow, but remained still as warmth tingled through my battered face. *Didn't your sister tell you not to heal me?*

Her eyes widened. *Were you eavesdropping again?*

I shifted my gaze to the side. *It's not my fault,* I declared defensively. *How am I supposed to ignore you when the two of you are chattering in my head? Hmmm?*

No one else can hear us, she argued, lifting her hand once she was satisfied my brain was in fact sound and not concussed.

You sure about that? I questioned, causing her nose to crinkle. *Also, do not ever refer to anything I do as **wolfy**.* I grimaced just thinking the word and her eyes brightened in amusement. I nodded to the open cell door. *Do you think it's a good idea for you to be in here?*

Paige rolled her eyes. *Honestly, you're as bad as Dru.*

I've heard worse insults.

I wanted to check on you.

She refused to talk to you, I guessed and the air gusted out of her. *I'm not sure I can help you.*

It's not me I want you to help, she retorted, staring at me pointedly.

I'm not giving up on her, I assured Paige. *But she doesn't seem exactly eager to leave.*

Paige looked at the ground. *It's my fault.*

I know. Her gaze shot to mine and I shrugged. *Wasn't exactly hard to figure out. You're the only thing she loves.*

She raised me. She's protected me every single day of my life. Paige crossed her arms over her chest. *But she's sacrificed everything for me.* Her eyes pleaded for understanding. *I know a wolf needs a pack.*

I'm not sure your sister knows that, I murmured, more to myself than Paige. *I'm pretty sure she's not going to leave, not without you.*

Paige frowned. *I was afraid you would say that.* She waved her hand. *You just need to convince her. You're her mate. Make her.*

I leaned back against the wall, shaking my head. *It doesn't work that* way. I grimaced, *Plus, I don't want a relationship like that.* I gestured to the door. *Why don't you leave with us?* She froze, not answering and I sighed. *I thought we were past all the secrets.*

Depends on the secret, she replied. *That one is mine.*

Well at the moment, it affects your sister…and me.

Just get her to leave, Paige begged with an intensity that made me study her more closely.

Why? I asked, her urgency contagious. *Why now? Why me? What do you think will happen?*

Gran will kill her, Paige said simply. *It's only a matter of time.*

Why do you think she'll kill her? I questioned, feeling a little desperate. *After all these years?*

I didn't expect Paige's next words. *Gran is determined to destroy the wolf inside of Dru.*

But that would kill Dru, I sputtered, dumbfounded.

Yes, but Gran can't see that. She blames the wolf for everything. And if she succeeds it'll be too late. Paige's eyes glistened. *I won't be able to heal Dru from a wound that severe.*

Her words made me question how many times she'd already healed Dru and any sympathy I might have felt for her grandmother disappeared. *The wolf is part of her. A part of her identity.* Paige nodded reluctantly. Pressure built in my chest at the thought of having the wolf taken from me. I couldn't imagine what it would do to Dru. She'd spent years relying on her wolf for survival, and if losing her wolf didn't kill her physically, it would break her mentally and emotionally. *I don't know how to convince her to leave, but I won't let your grandmother hurt her,* I promised Paige, and seeing the hope bloom in her eyes my resolve hardened. I had no idea how I was going to uphold my promise but knowing what the stakes were, I knew I would do whatever it took.

Chapter Nine

Dru

Paige? I called out mentally as I dropped onto the bed. She didn't answer and I flopped back on the bed, exhaustion tugging at me. I touched my lips, remembering the way they tingled when I brushed them against Caleb's. "You're a fool," I announced to the empty room, the words echoing in the cold air. It was so cold I could see my breath which didn't faze me, but Paige felt the cold more keenly.

I forced myself up, but didn't bother with shoes as I padded outside and collected firewood. I set more logs on the fire, then stirred the coals until flames flickered to life, warming the air.

You called? She appeared in the doorway, her jacket still on.

Where have you been? I questioned sharply and her expression became guarded. *Paige*, I sighed. *Caleb isn't some magical knight in shining armor. He's just a man.*

He's a shifter, Paige corrected me, like I didn't know that better than she ever could. *And you're the one who called him Captain America.*

Because of his looks! I said, exasperated. *Not because he's some hero who's going to save the day.*

You don't know that, Paige protested, snagging one of the comics off the nightstand we shared. *Why do you read these if you don't believe? At least a little bit?* Her face pleaded with me to agree, but I only shook my head.

They were Dad's, I answered, taking the comic book back and setting it gently on the stack. She scrutinized me, seeing everything I didn't want her to see. *You need to stop talking to Caleb*, I warned her. *It's too dangerous.*

If she kills him, you're not going to be okay, Paige stated and my chest tightened painfully. *See? Just saying it pains you.*

It's just the stupid mating thing, I argued, dismissing her words. I tapped the bite mark on my lip. *Heal it and I'll be fine.*

I don't think it works that way, Paige disagreed, staring at me sadly.

We won't know until you try.

She reached over, placing her finger against my lip, but the familiar warmth never came. I glanced at her, but she shrugged helplessly. *It's not a wound I can heal*, she answered, her mouth pinching worriedly. *Why didn't Caleb escape when he had the chance?*

He wouldn't leave without me, I grumbled, trying to hide the tiny spurt of pleasure that thought brought me. I'd spent years being the strong one, relying on no one because there had never been anyone, and now he'd shown up and was refusing to leave, and I was the reason.

And why didn't you go with him? Paige prodded and I gave her a cross look.

I'm not leaving you, I stated, shaking my head adamantly. *You know this.*

Paige's eyes darkened as she frowned. *I'm not a child anymore. I can take care of myself.*

I know you can. There was no mistaking her surprise at my agreement. *But leaving you at her mercy isn't an option.* My expression tightened. *I can't do it.* I'd spent too many years acting as a buffer between Paige and Gran, and the idea of leaving my little sister defenseless was abhorrent to me.

I'm not completely defenseless, Paige retorted and I blinked, not realizing I'd pushed that thought to her. *I'm as powerful as Gran.*

That startled a laugh out of me. *The fact that you think so is enough reason for me to stay.* A hurt expression crossed her face, sobering me. *You're strong, but in a different way, Paige.* I clasped her hand, grateful when she didn't jerk away. *You heal, and it is a powerful gift, but never underestimate Gran.*

I don't, she snapped, standing up, and my hands dropped away from hers. *You are the one who underestimates her.*

I sat back, surprised by her outburst. *I know exactly how powerful she is,* I contended and some of the steam left Paige as she dropped back on the bed, shaking her head.

I'm not talking about power, she answered tiredly.

Then what are we talking about? I asked in confusion.

Intention, Paige replied, one shoulder lifting then dropping. Her casual demeanor belied her next words. *She intends to rip the wolf right out of your body and if you think I can fix that, then you overestimate my ability.*

I lowered my head, my amber eye twitching at Paige's interpretation of the situation. I started to shake my head and the weight of her sigh ruffled my hair.

I'm not stupid, Dru.

She's never succeeded, I protested weakly, not needing to see her irritated expression to know exactly how ridiculous my argument was.

Not for lack of trying, Paige countered waspishly. *She can't see past her anger and you can't see past your guilt.* My head snapped up and she bit her lip. *I shouldn't have said that.*

Why? You're right, I admitted thickly. *If our parents were alive, everything would be different.*

We can't know that, Paige reminded me. *It might have been worse.* I gave her a cynical stare. *Okay, it probably wouldn't have been worse, but we can't think about that. All we have is the here and now.*

And right now, it's my job to protect you, I declared, standing abruptly. *You deserve a life.*

Paige's smile was brittle. *And you don't?* She waved her arm around the room we'd shared our entire life, the rough log walls barely adequate in the cold winters. *There is no life to be had here*, she said, saying what we both knew but rarely acknowledged. *No future. No love. No job. Nothing. This place is dying.*

Her words unleashed a torrent of emotions, the strongest being bitter regret. *Are you okay?* Caleb's voice caught me off guard and I sat down as waves of cold and hot flashed through my body at the unexpected concern he expressed for my wellbeing. His arrival had taken me by surprise. I'd never expected to meet anyone like him, to care about anyone besides my sister, or to want to feel responsible for another person, and then he'd shown up.

I'm fine, I replied automatically and a shiver went through me as I *felt* his doubt, but he didn't question me, a fact I was grateful for as I met Paige's eyes. *You're right*, I told her, *About all of it*, I continued with a sigh as her eyes widened in surprise. *Staying isn't an option, but neither is leaving you.*

She smiled sadly. *I can't leave and you won't go.* I gripped her hand, any comfort I attempted to give futile in the face of our reality. *I'd hoped one of us would have a chance at a life*, Paige murmured. She bumped the stack of old comics intentionally. *That heroes really did exist.*

I didn't like seeing her hopeless expression but before I could say anything, there was a knock at the door. I moved silently, pausing at the door until Paige nodded, the glow fading from her eyes. The heavy wooden latch thudded against the wall as I cracked the door. Margaret's eyes met mine for the barest second before she looked down, her head bowed.

"Miss, do you have any more of the deer meat?" Her voice quavered, as did most of the villagers whenever they had to come to me.

I shook my head, then frowned when I realized she couldn't see me because her eyes were glued to the floor. "No, where's Strickland?" I asked brusquely, almost all requests for food or resources went through Strickland at Gran's request. Most of the villagers were terrified of me, so she must be desperate.

"I don't know," she whispered, almost crying. "I can't find him."

My forehead wrinkled at that information and Paige came to the door. *You're scaring her*, she reprimanded, brushing me aside.

I didn't do anything, I protested as the door creaked open wider. *I just asked a simple question.*

Paige reached for Margaret's hands and when she realized who it was she looked up in relief. Paige patted her hands gently, smiling through gritted teeth as she asked me, *What does she want?*

Meat, I answered, buffing my nails on my shirt. *Strickland isn't around.*

They're hungry, Paige concluded, still smiling as she raised her hand, mimicking eating and Margaret nodded hopefully. *Do we have anything?*

I leaned back, out of Margaret's line of sight as I shook my head.

Nothing? Paige asked a little desperately and I lifted my shoulders helplessly.

We're all hungry, I reminded her unnecessarily. Food was scarce since most animals avoided our land, sensing it was tainted and there were no roads, making trips into towns difficult at best, and near impossible during the winter.

She has a sick son, Paige prompted and I closed my eyes, already well aware of that fact. *We can't let her leave emptyhanded.*

I cursed under my breath, knowing she was right, but not liking my options. *Give her our dinner*, I told her and Paige's eyes shot to mine, already knowing what was coming. *I'll have to go hunt tonight.*

It's dangerous, Paige replied, grabbing for my arm, but I was already at the window.

So is starving, I muttered grimly, raising the sash and slipping out so Margaret wouldn't see me.

One meal won't hurt anything, Paige called after me, worried, and I glanced back.

Caleb has to eat, I said, feeling my stomach clench with hunger. I understood all too well the appetite of a shifter, the constant, gnawing hunger of an empty belly, and if he had any hope of surviving then he'd need meat. *I'll be back soon*, I reassured her, but the pinched look didn't leave her face as I ducked my head, making my way to the woods.

I hadn't gone two miles when I felt the link I shared with Caleb flare to life. *Where are you going?* I slowed, my concentration split between Caleb and the ground, as I tried to avoid long ago set traps.

Why do you think I'm going somewhere? I asked instead of answering.

I felt you shift.

I stumbled in surprise. *You felt me shift?*

Yeah, it hurts, he grunted, something in his tone telling me he wasn't pleased about that fact. *Then it felt like you were moving away from me.*

That I understood. Our connection felt like a thin string, growing taut as the distance between us grew. *I need to hunt*, I answered briefly, my hackles rising slightly. I didn't like this feeling of having to account for my whereabouts.

Need? He prodded and a low growl escaped me. My stride lengthened as I tried to outrun the connection. *Dru*, his voice took on a soothing note, *I worry about you. I'm stuck in a cage. Help me understand.*

I snorted, shaking my head but I slowed down and it felt like the connection between us grew more elastic, allowing it to stretch further. *In case you haven't noticed, there's not a lot of stores around here.*

A spurt of amusement met my words. *Are there any?*

Nope. Which means hunting and gardening are the main sources of food. My steps grew eager as I approached the border of our land. I sniffed, picking up the scent of a rabbit. It wouldn't be enough to take home but it would ease the ache in my own stomach. *Problem is food is scarce. It was a bad growing season and most of the hunts are unsuccessful.*

Wolves hunt in packs, he mentioned casually and I gnashed my teeth.

It's not my ability, I retorted in irritation. *I have to go further to find meat*, I explained, reining in my anger as I pounced on my dinner. I tore into the rabbit, finishing it in seconds. *Every year there are less animals.*

Do you know why? I sensed his puzzlement. It would be difficult to over hunt the land since I was essentially the only predator around.

They sense the wrongness, I suggested and felt his unease. It matched my own. Every year the crops grew smaller and the hunts less successful. It was as if my mother's curse spread, contaminating every inch of the land. *The land is poisoned, cursed by grief.*

You can hunt our lands, he offered and I shook my head, ears flapping, even though he couldn't see.

No, I answered, zeroing in on a fresh trail. *We don't need your help.*

He hummed, but I didn't respond as I stalked my prey, unyielding on this point. *What's mine is yours*, he finally mentioned. *That's the way it is with mates.*

I hope that doesn't mean you expect me to share my dinner, I retorted, the wild boar coming into sight. A tingle of fear went through me as I watched the beast root in the dirt, its sharp tusks gleaming in the moonlight.

What are you hunting? Caleb questioned abruptly. *Dru*, he said sharply when I didn't answer immediately. *What are you hunting?*

Whatever is available, I said evasively.

That's not an answer. His growing concern pressed down on me. *I should be with you.*

You should be with your own Pack, I retorted, slinking forward. *Now be quiet so I can concentrate.* His emotions cut off abruptly, but I could still sense him with me, a Pack mate ready to offer assistance.

Boar, I answered and he cursed. A second later though, possible strategies flooded through the link, images of successful hunts, and I smiled, filing them away as I prepared to lunge, my best chance a surprise attack.

My teeth sank into tough hide and I immediately started to shake my head, trying to tear through as it squealed, twisting its body to get me off. I hung on, trying to avoid the sharp tusks and hooves. Blood made it slippery and my grip loosened, and the boar gave a hard shake and sent me skidding to the side. The boar trumpeted, not turning to run, but instead turning to charge me. I moved, but not fast enough as one of those sharp tusks pierced my side, and I twisted, using my claws to rip into its underbelly.

My teeth snapped at its neck, finally sinking in deep enough to do damage. I felt it start to weaken and clung, desperate to end the fight as blood oozed from my side. Luck wasn't with me though as a snuffling snort broke through the clearing, and another boar trotted into view. I started to back away, dragging the dying boar with me, not prepared to take on another one.

It stopped, sniffing the air, its beady eyes focusing on me, and I prayed it would turn and go the other way. It scratched the ground and I dropped the boar clamped between my jaws as the latest one charged me.

Get behind it, Caleb directed and I obeyed, leaping over the charging boar. *Attack it from behind.*

I twisted, nipping at the boar's hind leg, hearing it squeal as my teeth broke bone.

Gut it.

My claws tore through its belly, feeling a hoof shatter one of my ribs but I didn't stop, knowing this was my only chance. I kicked with my back legs, sending it slamming against a tree, a loud crack telling me its spine had snapped.

I collapsed on the ground, blood seeping faster from where the tusk had gotten me, and each breath was harder than the last as the bone from my shattered rib pressed on my lungs.

Shift, Caleb instructed, *shift before you bleed out.*

I blinked, the trees blurring as the pain started to fade.

Dru, a voice yelled. *Dru, shift now. Dru, please.* His panic plucked at me, sharpening my focus. *If you don't shift you'll die.*

That didn't sound so bad, I thought to myself.

It's very bad, he replied desperately. *I need you. Paige needs you.*

Her name sent a jolt through me, and a hiss escaped me as pain pierced through the numbness.

That's it, come on, Princess. Fight. Strength filled me, first a trickle and then a flood as I felt the force of his will through the connection we shared. *Do not leave me*, he ordered and my nose twitched at the command. *You don't like that? Do something about it*, he dared, reading my emotions easily.

Anger spiked through me, the shift starting as my body struggled to heal itself, but when my body twisted, tendons and bones snapping, the pain overwhelmed me. A whimper escaped me as my mind fought the agonizing pain, unable to tell where it came from, and my connection to Caleb grew weak.

Give it to me, the words were barely a whisper but I clung to them desperately, lost to the pain, as I finally let go.

***

Minutes, or maybe hours later, I woke up, curled on the ground, my side throbbing, my skin slick with blood. I sat up gingerly, favoring the side with the shattered rib, knowing it hadn't healed properly. The clearing looked like a war zone, with blood splattered everywhere, and I stood, swaying slightly as I made my way to the dead boar. Satisfaction surged through me at seeing them dead and I flipped one of them over with my foot.

Hazy memories drifted through my mind as I stared at the bloody tusk of the boar. I shivered, remembering the cold numbness that had spread through me, and the deep voice that had kept me from drifting away. I poked through my thoughts but couldn't sense Caleb.

"Caleb?" I said aloud, not sure how to make him hear me. *Caleb?* I tried again, internally this time. There was no answer and I fought a sense of unease. "Maybe I'm too far away," I told myself, the words echoing in the clearing. *Paige?*

OH MY GOD, where have you been? She shrieked and my eye twitched at the volume. *It's been hours. I was worried sick.* She paused and my gaze swept the area, trying to ignore my growing concern. *Are you okay?*

Yeah, I replied automatically, my thoughts elsewhere, until I bent down and pain spiked through me. *I might need a little healing*, I amended, breathing shallowly as black dots danced in my vision.

Seriously, what happened? Worry bled through our bond as I forced myself upright.

I killed dinner, I answered, downplaying how dangerous the hunt had actually been. *Now I just have to figure out how to get it home.*

Then why do you need me to heal you? She hummed suspiciously. *Usually you can heal yourself.*

One of my ribs broke, I said dismissively, pulling some vines out of the trees to tie up the boar's legs. I was going to have to drag them out because there was no way I was leaving any meat behind. *Can you go check on Caleb?* I asked, deflecting her attention from me.

Why do I need to check on him? You're the one that's hurt.

And when I get back, you'll fix me up. Until then, go check on Caleb, I responded tartly, cradling my side as I leaned against the tree, fighting the urge to throw up and pass out at the same time. Pain was a familiar companion, but it never got any easier.

You're worried about him, she decided, understanding dawning. *You care about him*, she accused and I closed my eyes, hating to admit she might be right. He'd saved my life, taken away the pain so I could shift, and the fact that he wasn't there when I'd woken up….it terrified me.

Checking on him will give you something to do so you won't badger me until I'm back, I retorted, kneeling so I could tie the boars together to make them easier to drag out of the forest.

Uh huh, and what do you think might happen to him in his jail cell? Paige questioned sardonically and I paused as several possible scenarios played in my mind, freezing on one where Gran stood before him, her eyes glowing brightly as she tried to separate the wolf from the man. *Okay, that would be bad*, Paige admitted, some of the sarcasm draining from her voice. *I'll check.* She paused. *Do you need me to come help you?*

No, I answered instantly and there was a second's worth of hurt before the emotion was muffled. *No, I need you to check on Caleb, please*, I requested, trying to smooth the unintentional hurt caused by my knee jerk reaction. The idea of Paige out here, in the woods….I looked down at the dead boar and let out a shaky breath. Paige was powerful but she wasn't a killer, a fact that could easily get her killed.

I will, she promised softly and I breathed easier. *Be careful, Dru.*

You too, little sister, I murmured, finishing the knots. Every step promised to be a special hell, but I was determined to get my kill home since it would feed them for at least a couple of weeks. I wrapped the vines around my wrist and started walking, my arm flexing as I met resistance and the boars bumped over the ground behind me. I kept my other arm tight against my side, trying to keep from jostling the shattered bone that hadn't been able to heal with the shift.

I hadn't made it a dozen steps when I had to stop, sweat breaking out on my lip. I slumped against a tree, each breath a struggle as the vines I was using as a rope dropped from my wrist. Weakness sent a tremble coursing through me. I brushed the back of my hand against my mouth, swallowing hard.

This wasn't normal.

That was my only thought as my knees gave out and I collapsed on the ground, my rib no longer my concern as my strength drained from me. I managed to roll onto my back, desperate to see the sky above me, if these were to be my last moments. I stared through the bare limbs of the trees to where the stars glittered in the night sky. Something ran down my temple and my finger shook as I touched the skin. My finger came away wet and I stared at the droplet as another ran into my hair, and realized I was crying.

I didn't understand what was happening to me, nothing Gran had ever done had come close to the paralyzing weakness that had overtaken me now, but as I lay there only one regret overwhelmed me.

Caleb.

His name whispered across my mind as the night sky blurred above me.

Dru.

My breath hitched at his faint response.

You're here, I murmured, as the tight band squeezing my chest eased.

Wouldn't be anywhere else, he answered glibly, too glibly as his voice caught. *What do you see?*

Stars. They're blanketing the sky.

Are they as stunning as you?

Far more stunning than I could ever be, I replied, warmth curling through me at his compliment.

Somehow I doubt that.

Apprehension crept in as I noted how pale his voice sounded. *Caleb*, I urged, panic piercing the lethargy taking over my body. *What's wrong?*

I need to break the connection between us, he mumbled indistinctly. *It might....hurt a bit.*

Why? I cried, struggling to sit up but too weak to move more than a couple of inches. *What's happening?*

Nothing, he tried to reassure me, but his voice faded in and out. *You'll be safe.*

What about you? The stars magnified as tears pooled in my eyes, my body growing numb while I waited for his reply.

White hot heat seared through me, arching my back as my brain felt like it was being carved into pieces and I heard Caleb's voice in the clearing, clear as a bell, "Stay safe, Princess."

"Caleb," I gasped, the worst pain of my life hitting me as it felt like my head was being split open. I rolled over, puking into the damp leaves, my mind terrifyingly silent. I laid there for several minutes, each heartbeat sending agony spiking through my head, until one heartbeat it hurt a little less, then another, and my fingers managed to curl into my palm.

"Caleb," I didn't recognize my voice, it was so rough and hoarse, and thought I must have been screaming without realizing it. "Caleb." He didn't answer and my temple throbbed in time to the beat of my heart. I sat up, swaying as some of my strength returned.

Moisture ran down my face and I swiped angrily at the tears that dared to fall, but when I looked at my hands, one was covered in blood. I reached up, touching the corner of my amber eye and when I pulled my finger back it was coated in blood. I touched my blue eye, but came away with only a single clear droplet.

"What did you do?" I muttered, struggling to my feet, my naked body coated in sticky blood and leaves. "Caleb, what did you do?" I screamed, but my voice was gone, the scream barely a whimper and I stumbled, falling against a tree as my feet wobbled. My body felt awkward, heavy, and almost useless, each motion as new as if I'd just learned it. I stepped forward, determined to find Caleb and force him to undo whatever it was he'd done, unable to deal with the empty echo of my own thoughts, his comforting presence far more apparent now that it was gone.

A snapping branch brought my head up, and instinct took over. I scuttled backwards, grabbing the dead boar and using the darkness to hide me as I curled into the hollow of a dead tree.

"You heard it." I recognized Strickland's voice and settled deeper into the tree's trunk, curious as to why he was out here and who was with him.

A voice I didn't know blustered, "Some animal dying. Why are we searching for it?"

"I don't want to find it," another voice squeaked, sounding suitably creeped out.

"If there's something out here I want to know what it is, besides that didn't sound like no animal," Strickland answered. "It sounded human."

"Again, I don't see why we need to find it."

"There's traps out here," Strickland reported. "One of 'em might have caught something." He paused and I held my breath. "Like a wolf shifter."

The other man grunted, but his steps fell more heavily on the ground. I glanced at the two boars I'd killed and quickly untied the vines wrapped around them. I dragged one further away, smearing blood along the ground, then positioned the other one on the edge of the clearing.

"What if it escaped? And attacks us?" The scared one questioned, his voice so high I winced. "I don't want to become no werewolf."

"It doesn't work that way, boy," the other one sneered. "Now shut up before you piss yourself."

I crouched, easing backwards, my gaze sweeping the area to make sure there was no sign of my presence. The vines caught my attention and I hurriedly shoved them deeper into the hollow. My breath hissed out as I heard them come closer and I looked for another place to hide.

My gaze caught on a low hanging limb and I swung myself up before I could change my mind. My rib protested, but there was no time as they came into the clearing. Silently, I braced myself against the trunk of the tree, trusting the darkness and their stupidity to keep me hidden.

"If there's traps out here, how do we know we won't step on one?" The kid's nervous question stopped them in their tracks and the older one shoved the younger one in front of him.

"Why don't you go first then?" He ordered as Strickland brought up the rear, his gaze wary. The kid stumbled into the clearing, his panicked gaze darting everywhere as he panted, practically hyperventilating. I tucked myself closer to the tree, afraid he might actually catch sight of me with the way his head was bobbing.

"Where is it?" The older man snarled. "A wolf can fetch a good price even if it's injured."

Strickland came up when he realized there was no injured wolf about to attack. My lip curled at the sight of him and this evidence of his betrayal. It wasn't hard to determine the two men were hunters and it appeared he was working with them.

"I don't see anything," the kid commented, his voice quavering. "Can we go now?"

Strickland pushed to the front, his gaze determined. "Something made that noise and I want to know what."

"Go ahead," the other guy muttered, yanked the kid back. "If it isn't a wolf shifter, I don't care."

He poked Strickland in the chest, his voice full of warning, "Just make sure you deliver what you promised or we'll have a problem."

"What's that?" My attention jerked back to the kid, afraid he'd spotted me, but he was pointing at the edge of the clearing where the boar's tuck was barely visible. "Is that a demon?"

The older guy rolled his eyes, shoving him aside as he stomped over to the dead boar. "No, boy. Your momma needs to quit filling your head with that foolishness." He kicked the dead animal. "Here's your human," he sneered to Strickland. "It's a dead pig."

"What killed it?" The kid asked, glancing around fearfully. "What could kill *that*?" I closed my eyes, cursing the damn kid and his incessant questions. Clearly, he was the only one with a brain.

His question made the other men draw up short as they traded wary glances. "Spread out, look for tracks," the older one ordered and Strickland shot him an angry look, but obeyed.

The kid wandered close to my tree, practically standing underneath it and I prayed he didn't look up because there was no way he would miss me. "Over here," Strickland called and the kid shuffled away as I let out the breath I'd been holding. "There's another one."

"Two of 'em must have fought. Killed each other."

"That would explain the noises we heard." The older man grabbed the kid. "Satisfied? I don't like wasting my time."

"Yeah," Strickland replied, nodding to the north. "Head that way about a mile and you'll be off our land." I gritted my teeth when he said *our land*. "There's no traps, but I'd avoid the lands to the south." My forehead wrinkled as Strickland warned the hunters away from Caleb's Pack lands. The other men muttered agreements, striding off as Strickland stood over the dead boars, and I held my breath, wondering what he would do next.

He waited until they were out of earshot, then leaned down and picked up a boar, slinging it over his shoulder then grabbing the other one. He lumbered into the woods in the direction of home and I exhaled, relief turning my body liquid. I sat heavily on the branch, trying to process what I'd just witnessed.

"Strickland is working with hunters." Even saying it out loud didn't help, the idea was so ludicrous. He'd been Gran's most loyal solider as long as I'd been alive. The idea that he would betray her seemed impossible, but there was no denying what I'd just seen.

I lowered myself out of the tree, catching my breath as I landed, my rib protesting the movement. I needed to get home, have Paige heal my rib, and find out what the hell Caleb had done.

Chapter Ten

Caleb

Agony racked my body, ten thousand times worse than the first time I'd experienced Dru shift, and I curled into a ball, desperately trying to hold onto my sanity. Finally, the pain started to recede, but phantom aches continued to radiate through me. Muscles cramped as I tried to stretch my legs out and I winced, unable to comprehend that Dru went through this every time she shifted.

I'd never really considered the magic of the shift. I'd always known it healed almost any wound but never realized the hidden effects. Taking the pain from Dru taught me differently and I had a new appreciation for her strength.

I propped myself up on my elbow, searching for my connection to her, and blew out a relieved breath when the warm ember of her life glowed brightly in my mind. I'd almost lost her to a damn boar attack, a risk she never should have taken on her own. Understanding why she had done it didn't make it any easier knowing she could have died.

I managed to haul myself upright, leaning against the cold stone wall, remembering the way I'd been able to see the fight through her eyes. It wasn't unusual for pack mates to be able relieve a memory or share an experience, but my bond with Dru wasn't complete and she wasn't technically a Pack mate. The strength of my connection to her was on par with the one I shared with Dom and it didn't make sense, but it didn't change the fact that she was becoming the most important person in my life.

Footsteps came down the stairs, each one deliberate, and the hair on my arms raised. I stood, recognizing the scent and unwilling to face her from a position of weakness. "It's good to see you again."

There was the barest hesitation as she came down the last step and her expression was unsmiling as she spoke, "A well-mannered wolf then."

"I would consider myself a well-mannered shifter," I replied, keeping my eyes on her as she moved further into the room, the bars a poor separation as I felt the immense power radiating from her.

"Bow," she commanded and my spine bent unwillingly. "Struggle only makes it harder on you," she commented, unable to even pretend sympathy. "You'll break….like all the rest."

"Like Dru?" Her power rippled at my question and I took advantage, straightening my back.

The blue of her eyes electrified as she hissed, "You dare speak her name as if you know her?" She stalked closer, pushing her will with every step and my knees buckled. "Her name is Drusilla Primrose Sinclair. She is descended of the original blood and you will *not* refer to her as *Dru*." Her chest heaved and her eyes glittered with rage as power pulsed from her and it was all I could do not to collapse under the force of it. "Insolent pup. You will learn to respect your creator."

I braced my hands against the floor, nausea rolling through me as I fought against her will. The sound of my ragged breaths filled the room and I spat, determined not to break under her sharp gaze. "I'll call her whatever she allows me to," I gritted out. "She has the right to her name."

She inhaled, and I choked as it felt like all the oxygen in the room disappeared. "But you have no rights here and I'm tired of your defiance." I managed to lift my head in time to see her smile icily. "Shift."

There was no resisting her command as my body shimmered, and a moment later my wolf stood there, a low growl escaping as I glared at her impotently. I snapped my teeth at her and she cocked her head.

"Shift."

Again, I couldn't stop the transformation as she commanded my body. I landed on my stomach and this time it was a little harder to push myself up.

"What are you doing?" I questioned, muscles quivering as I held myself off the ground.

"Solving a problem," she answered and this time she didn't bother to utter a command before I was once again a wolf. My head hung low as I panted, trying to figure out how she could force the shift on me, something I thought only an Alpha could do.

"How?" I grunted when I was once again a man. I stayed on the ground, conserving my strength, and she sighed.

"They don't teach you the origins of your kind?"

I shook my head slightly and she moved until her feet stood in front of my face.

"Pity. You might have thought twice about coming here if you'd known."

I anticipated the shift this time but even with the small window of opportunity, I couldn't stop it from happening. My wolf couldn't stand and we laid there, our energy depleted to frighteningly low levels.

"Still you fight me." She almost sounded impressed, but I wasn't encouraged. "You are strong." Her teeth flashed. "The harder you are to break, the longer it'll take," she crooned as I once again laid there as a man. I couldn't recall how many times I'd shifted in a row, but it was too many.

"Stop," I ordered and she let a startled laugh.

"You think you can command me?" I could hear her move, but couldn't open my eyes. "You should thank me for your very existence," she snapped and I managed to crack my eyes open a slit. "Without us, you wouldn't exist."

She forced me to shift twice in rapid succession and what little strength I had disappeared. I couldn't even twitch a finger, but what terrified me was how dim my connection to Dru had grown. I barely felt her energy at all.

I could feel another shift coming and desperation gave me the strength to resist it. I was horrified to realize I'd been draining strength from Dru through our connection.

"What are you doing, wolf?" I heard her screech but withdrew into my mind, conserving my last bit of energy to do what I needed to save Dru.

Caleb, Dru's soft voice came through, full of regret, but if was the last thing I heard I'd die a happy man.

Dru, I replied and her warmth blanketed me, disguising the fact that I was freezing.

You're here, she breathed and something loosened in my chest.

Wouldn't be anywhere else, I answered smoothly, not wanting to worry her. A surge of power went through me as her Gran tried to force the shift again, and as I resisted my voice cracked when I asked, *What do you see?*

Stars. They're blanketing the sky, she answered, barely audible as her strength waned along with mine.

Are they as stunning as you? I asked, already knowing she outshined them all.

Far more stunning than I could ever be, she replied, but I could sense her pleasure at my comparison.

Somehow I doubt that, I contended, my voice fading as I fought the power slamming into me. Each second was harder to hold than the last and I wasn't sure how much longer I could do it.

Caleb, Dru's panicked voice fueled my determination. *What's wrong?*

I need to break the connection between us, I answered, hearing my words slur. I didn't have much time and I knew she wouldn't be able to sever the bond. *It might....hurt a bit,* I lied, knowing it would be the worst agony imaginable, but also aware she was strong enough to withstand the abrupt loss of a Pack bond.

Why? She cried out, and I sensed her trying to reach me. *What's happening?*

Nothing, I lied again, unwilling to tell her that her grandmother was slowly killing me and it was killing Dru as well because we were linked. Only one thing mattered and it was my strongest thought, *You'll be safe.*

What about you? Her words blurred, unintelligible, as another surge of power threatened to take me. I knew there was no more time and I had to sever the bond between us now. With my next breath, I let go, mouthing the words I prayed she could somehow hear, "Stay safe, Princess."

Words couldn't describe the next moments, my thoughts scattered as I tried to remember who I was without her. The Pack bond I shared with Dom and the Navarre Pack flickered dangerously, threatening to extinguish and I knew once it was gone I would be lost. Breaking the bond I shared with Dru was worse than releasing my Pack and position of Alpha.

It was worse than dying.

The only thing that allowed me to endure the loss was knowing it was the one thing that could save her.

"Wolf, you will not escape me," Dru's grandmother screamed, spittle flying, and my eyes flew open. The Pack bond I shared with the Navarre Pack brightened, then glowed white hot as they reached out, sensing my loss and protecting me.

I rolled into a crouch, one fist planted on the ground as I stared her down, my wolf fierce behind my eyes as I growled, "She's safe now. Do your worst, witch."

The blast of power slammed me against the wall, my skull cracking loudly and I slid down the wall, my vision blurred as I looked at her, rage contorting her face, her hands held out as if she could ring the life from me. Everything stared to fade, my injuries fatal if I didn't shift, but my body couldn't go through another shift.

My eyes started to close, unwilling to have my last vision be of the bitter woman who choose to kill me, when I saw her fold and fall to the ground, as a white angel took her place.

***

Don't die, a sweet voice begged. *Don't tell me I was too late. Dru is going to kill me.* My heart pounded, thoughts slowing congealing, one word echoing above the others, Dru. *Yes, yes, that's it. Oh thank God.* She kept talking, the words scrambling around in my head, but I didn't try to make sense of them. A keen sense of loss pierced me and I reached, trying to find the cause for the huge hole in my mind.

Pack. The thought consumed me.

We can get you to your Pack, a frantic voice assured me. *Just wake up and tell me where they are. Oh God, preferably before she wakes up.*

A tiny light flared to life, its light comforting me, but not explaining the deep sorrow I continued to feel.

Dru will be here soon.

Dru, I repeated, latching onto the name as sorrow sent a sharp pang through me. She was the reason I felt this way.

Yes, Dru, the voice answered, sounding relieved and familiar. *Dru will know what to do.* The voice paused and I recognized it as female. *I hope.*

I pried my eyes open a crack, but could only see a curtain of white. The curtain parted and insanely blue eyes met mine. *You're awake,* a surge of relief shot through me, but I knew it wasn't mine. Those eyes began to glow as heat snaked through my head. *You're hurt but I can't tell where,* she told me, her lips pressed together in concentration. *Can you tell me where it hurts?*

Paige, I stated and she nodded, giving me an encouraging look.

Yes, I'm Paige. It's good you know who I am. Stress lines bracketed her mouth, aging her, and I tried to pat her hand, but fell short.

I'm okay, I tried to reassure her, but she only gave me a doubtful stare. *I promise.*

I can feel your pain, she explained, her eyebrows drawing down. *I just can't find its source.*

Some wounds you can't heal, I informed her, knowing the pain she referred to was the loss of my bond with Dru. She lifted her hands from my head, and sat back on her heels, studying me. *You just have to live with them.* Memories and thoughts pieced themselves back together, reminding me who I was, and I dragged myself into a sitting position.

Where is Dru? I asked, unable to reach her mentally even though I had no problem communicating with Paige. I slumped forward, fighting the weakness that plagued me, but it was impossible.

She's on her way back, Paige assured me. *She's just not here yet.*

My gaze caught on the crumpled form of Paige's Gran and I asked, *What happened?* Paige's eyes widened as she gave me a frightened look and I shook my head. *I'm not going to be mad*, I told her, really hoping the old bat was dead.

I....., Paige stopped, staring at me like she hoped I could just read her mind so she wouldn't have to say it out loud.

You have to tell me, I prompted, switching my gaze from Gran lying there to Paige.

I hit her, Paige answered, the words barely a whisper in my mind.

I nodded, impressed despite myself. *Why did you come?* I asked, puzzled by her presence.

Dru sent me, Paige rocked back on her heels. *I was almost too late.*

But you weren't too late, I told her and nodded to Gran. *And you saved my life.*

Paige bobbed her head, wrapping her arms around herself as she looked over her shoulder at her grandmother. *But she's going to wake up eventually*, she finally answered and I winced, no longer ignorant of her Gran's ability. *Then what do we do?*

I didn't have an answer for her as I shuddered with cold, unable to regulate my body temperature. Paige saw and seemed to realize the problem. She gathered the few clothes lying around and handed them to me. *What do you need?*

Food, I grimaced at the gnawing sensation in my stomach. *A lot of it.*

She shot me an apologetic glance and shook her head. *Dru is supposed to bring meat.* Paige rubbed her hands together. *There's never enough to go around.*

How many? She gave me a confused look and I clarified. *How many live here?*

22, she answered.

They don't provide food? I questioned and she glanced down. *They don't share the responsibility?*

They're old mostly. There are a couple younger than me, but if they could leave they did, she explained. *There are no jobs here, and Gran is,* we both glanced over at the old woman on the ground, still formidable even when she was down, *Gran,* Paige finished with an audible gulp.

And you won't explain why you won't leave?

Paige grew thoughtful, but before she could say anything we heard shouting. She scrambled to her feet and shot me a frightened look. *They can't find her here like this.*

No one is going to come down here, I assured her. *Go find out what's going on.*

She raced out of the cell, forgetting to shut it and I slowly got to my feet, my gaze locked on the helpless form of Gran.

Chapter Eleven

Dru

I jogged the last mile, feeling a sense of urgency coming from Paige. Caleb was a blank page in my mind, and frustration warred with worry as I came to the outskirts of our little community. Dawn was peeking over the horizon but already several members had gathered in the center of the village. I skirted around them, not wanting to be discovered coming from the woods completely naked and covered in my own blood.

What's going on? I asked Paige, heading for the house.

Where are you? She sounded freaked and I slowed, ready to change direction if she needed me.

Going to the house. I need clothes, I answered calmly.

I'll meet you there, she replied. *Strickland came back with two boars*, she added. *Did you have anything to do with that?*

I didn't reply, wishing for the umpteenth time that a conversation could end when you were no longer in earshot, instead of the mental ones that meant you couldn't escape. She didn't push though and I ducked into the crude outdoor shower, pulling the handle to dump freezing water over my head and rinse the blood off.

A towel appeared in the door and I took it, scrubbing myself dry. I lowered the towel to find

Paige scowling at me. *I'm fine*, I muttered and she rolled her eyes, her finger poking my side. I flinched, dodging another strike. *Okay, not completely fine.*

Her hand hovered over my side and I nodded, letting her heal the fractured rib. Heat radiated from her palm as the bone splintered apart and knitted back together correctly. I gritted my teeth against the pain but didn't utter a sound. *Caleb?* I questioned, unable to wait any longer.

He's alive, she reported, her eyes coming up to meet mine. *But we have another problem.*

I tilted my head and she motioned for me to follow her, tossing a shirt at me. I yanked it over my head as we headed back to the underground cell, avoiding the excited people gathered around the boars Strickland had brought back. *Never fails*, I muttered, watching as they congratulated him.

Quit pouting, Paige ordered.

I'm not pouting, I retorted, smoothing my expression before she turned around. *He just gets all the credit. Is it any wonder they despise me?*

Paige slowed, her gaze contrite. *They don't despise you,* she replied and I let out a disbelieving huff. *They're terrified of you,* she revealed, as if that was somehow a better alternative.

Thanks, that makes me feel so much better, I answered, casting a lingering glance at those who'd gathered before hurrying to catch up to Paige. *What is so –* I stopped, staring in disbelief. "Gran?" I hurried down the stone steps, a different kind of dread going through me at seeing her lying on the ground. "Is she?" I glanced at Paige but she didn't look any different, giving me hope that Gran hadn't kicked the bucket.

"She's alive," Caleb testified, relieving me of one fear. "Still out cold though. Paige whacked her good."

"Pa-," I couldn't even say her name as I stumbled to a stop. "You…" I pointed at Gran as I looked at Paige, forgetting for a moment that she couldn't hear me, but she clearly understood because her expression became remorseful.

I did it to save him, she defended, gesturing to Caleb.

"It's true," he confirmed and my gaze darted to him as he answered one of my questions. "Paige saved my life." He swallowed, his face worn, but his blue eyes shined brightly as he looked me over. "You're okay."

I nodded shallowly. "I've had better days." I took in his wan expression, the dark circles under his eyes and the way he held onto the wall. "But my day was still better than yours, I think."

She was killing him, Paige shouted and both of us winced. *Sorry*, she muttered as we turned to look at her. *I didn't know what you were saying.*

Caleb, I tried mentally, but he didn't react and I wasn't sure if it was because he didn't hear me or some other reason. "We'll talk later," I muttered, dismissing him as I turned back to Paige and Gran's unconscious body. *We need to get her home*, I told Paige, who nodded, her gaze darting between me and Caleb.

He's hungry, she squeaked and I heard an audible snap come from Caleb's direction. *And cold.* A rumble met that revelation and I glanced over my shoulder at him.

"She means well," I snapped, irritated that apparently he and Paige could communicate just fine. "I'll be back soon with food and clothes."

"I'm fine," he said curtly and I spun around, planting my hands on my hips.

"You're not fine," I contended, irrationally angry. "You just went a dozen rounds with Gran. You should be dead." My chest rose and fell as I tried to rein in my emotions and his gaze swept over me, taking in the shirt that barely hit mid-thigh and my filthy feet. "I think food and clothing aren't too much to ask for."

"But I didn't ask for them," he commented and my hand balled into a fist. "But I'll welcome anything you provide," he added hastily and I forcibly relaxed my hand. "You know I didn't mean to insult you…."

"Just shut up," I interrupted, reaching down and scooping Gran into a fireman's hold. "I'll be back soon with your gruel."

"I deserved that," he called as I stomped up the steps, Paige at my heels. "I'm sorry."

I paused at the top of the stairs, avoiding Paige as she almost ran into me, and looked down at him as he stood in front of the bars. "And what exactly are you sorry for?" I asked pointedly and he dropped his gaze. "I'll be back," I sighed, afraid to linger any longer with Gran. There was no telling when she might wake up and I had little desire to explain since I didn't even really understand what was going on.

I'm confused, Paige piped up and I grimaced.

That makes two of us.

I ducked into the shadows, adjusting my hold on Gran. *Do your thing, sister*, I murmured and she nodded, moving in front of us.

Why don't you levitate her? Paige questioned, walking slowly so the glamour she'd covered us with would look more natural, and anyone whose gaze came our way would just skip right past us.

This is just as easy, I dismissed, unwilling to admit that I couldn't access my abilities at the moment. My energy was at an all-time low and I suspected it had something to do with Caleb and whatever Gran had done. I was pretty sure a shift would be impossible and I was worried I wouldn't make it back to the cabin with Gran.

Almost there, Paige said, sounding relieved, and I didn't answer, concentrating on putting one foot in front of the other. She hurried to open the door and we slipped inside, grateful no one had stopped us. *Here*, Paige pushed Gran's door open and moved out of my way as I dropped her onto the bed, almost collapsing myself. *I've got you*, Paige murmured, hooking her arms underneath mine and pulling me up. We moved haltingly to the door, Paige supporting more of my weight than I was, when she stopped. *What about her?*

I glanced back at the bed where Gran sprawled inelegantly and knew we needed to cover our tracks.

Change her into her nightgown, tuck her under the covers, and pretend we have no idea what she's talking about when she asks, I finally said, my legs quivering under my own weight.

Can you make it into the kitchen? Paige questioned doubtfully, caught between me and Gran, and I nodded to make her decision easier.

There's nothing there to eat, but I can make it, I replied, attempting a smile, but it fell flat.

Paige smiled mysteriously as she said, *Second shelf on the left.* I eyeballed her but she didn't say anything more as I made my way to the kitchen, using the walls for support. I opened the cabinet she'd mentioned and almost squealed when I saw what she'd hidden there. I ripped the tin lid off the can and pulled out a Vienna sausage, popping it into my mouth, and moaned in satisfaction.

I demolished the can before she came in the room and she shook her head when she saw me licking my fingers. *Did you wash your hands at least?* My finger hovered next to my mouth as I gave her a sheepish look. She rolled her eyes and walked to the cabinet, digging deeper than I had. *Here.* She thrust a can of Spam at me and my eyes lit up. *For Caleb*, she stated and my mouth curled in a pout. *What's your deal with him?*

He broke a promise, I answered thoughtlessly, the sting sharper than I would have ever imagined. I'd been angry at him for creating the connection but now that he'd severed it without my consent I was....I exhaled, unsure how I felt.

You're sad, Paige noted as I leaned against the counter. Her eyes narrowed as she tilted her head. *And betrayed?* It came out as a question, but instead of explaining Caleb's role in my emotional state, I told her what I'd seen with Strickland.

He's working with hunters? Paige repeated, bumping into the table as she sank down onto a chair. *Strickland? Hunters?* She seemed as baffled as I had been by the knowledge, but anger quickly overtook her confusion. *Do you think…*her lips turned white as she pressed them together, eyeing me. *You?* She shook her head, quickly amending her half spoken question. *Do you think Strickland is planning to give you to the hunters?*

I shrugged, not liking the thought but….*Who else?*

Paige stood abruptly, her fists clenched as her hair started to swirl around her face and I leaned back, the counter preventing me from going far as her eyes glowed brighter than I'd ever witnessed, so bright they outshined Gran. *He can try*, she hissed, her normally clear voice almost guttural.

Whoa, sister. We don't know that for a fact…so maybe dial it down? Just a smidge, I held my fingers apart an inch, feeling her power pulsing in the air, so strong it was lifting my hair. It was easy to forget how strong Paige was, especially standing on family ground, where she could draw on our mother's power, a power she should have inherited directly if not for the method of our mother's death. She didn't relax and I raised my hands. *He's not going to win*, I told her. *He can't take me. We won't let it happen.*

Together, I gestured between us, *me and you, together forever, remember?*

Some of the tension eased from her face, and the strong scent of ozone started to fade as her power diminished slowly. *I could use a shot of that juice*, I joked, grabbing a glass from the counter and filling it with water to hide the faint trembling of my hand.

Paige could level the village if she wanted, a fact Gran seemed content to turn a blind eye to, but the possibility never left my mind, not with our mother's death etched in my memory.

Here. Her intention dawned on me a second too late as she touched my arm and a jolt shot through me. The sensation might be compared to sticking your finger in an electrical outlet except I'd never done that since we didn't have electricity. Generators were our main source of power and those weren't reliable or used every day, but the surge of power Paige sent through me would have been enough to light every house for a year.

Are you okay?

Her voice rang in my ears as I blinked, wooden logs dancing in my vision as I tried to figure out what I was seeing. Paige's face loomed over me and I realized I was on the floor and the dancing logs were the ceiling.

I'm alive....I think. My nose twitched at the overwhelming smell of gunpowder, and I touched my face gingerly, almost expecting it not to be there.

I didn't know that would happen, Paige cried out, her hands hovering over me as she tried to decide if touching me again was a good idea.

Ah, let's not, I suggested as she was about to pat my arm. My skin felt like it was crackling and energy coursed through me. It was almost as if she'd just charged my internal battery, except she'd almost fried the battery.

Oh, okay, she replied, tucking her hands under her armpits. *Sorry*. Remorse lined her face and I nodded reassuringly.

I'm fine, I lied adroitly. *Brings new meaning to being buzzed*. I stood up, quite positive I could fly if I wanted there was so much energy zipping through me. *You pack a punch, sister*. She frowned and I forced a soothing smile. *I'm gonna go check on Caleb*, I told her. *You stay here in case Gran wakes up*.

What do I tell her? Paige asked, her eyes filled with panic.

Nothing, I replied, giving her a warning stare. *You tell her nothing. You have no idea where she was, or what she was doing. As far as you know, she was in bed.*

You think she'll buy that, Paige asked doubtfully.

I shrugged. *She has no choice.* I walked to the door or possibly floated, since I wasn't sure my feet were touching the ground.

Don't forget his Spam, Paige reminded me and I hid a grimace, turning back around to pick up the can, almost afraid I'd fry the Spam right in the can when I touched it. *You're sure you're okay?*

Never better, I answered, my toes digging into the ground, an irresistible urge to run coming over me. *Now, go to bed,* I ordered and she saluted. I shut the door, then let my feet fly across the yard and I leaped over the remnants of a campfire, landing with a bounce. Energy flowed through me, disguising the fact that my belly was still hungry, and I'd almost died not once but twice that night.

I didn't bother to walk down the stairs, instead jumping and landing in a crouch right in front of Caleb's cell. His eyes popped open in surprise and I tossed the Spam to him. He caught it easily as I snapped my fingers. "I forgot clothes."

He peeled the lid off the Spam, digging into it with his fingers as he eyed me. "Sure that wasn't an intentional oversight?" Dirty pants hung low on his hips, highlighting the defined planes of his abdomen – muscles that were so well defined because he was starving and dehydrated.

"It wasn't," I assured him, dropping my gaze so I couldn't be accused of ogling him. He offered me the can and I shook my head.

"I ate," I informed him and his gaze skimmed over me.

"Not enough," he replied, finishing off the gelatinous meat mixture and tossing the can on the ground. "I'm sorry I broke our bond without warning," he said, surprising me. He came to the bars, hooking his wrists over them. "That wasn't fair of me." I moved my shoulder in a barely visible shrug, trying to pretend like it didn't matter and he shook his head. "I didn't want to do it."

"You were trying to save my life," I whispered, knowing it was true. He nodded. "Why does it hurt so much?"

He inhaled deeply, holding the breath for a long moment. "Because it's a Pack bond, a mating bond. They aren't taken lightly and they're important to our mental well-being."

"You knew it would hurt," I mentioned, fishing for information and finally he nodded.

"I've experienced it before."

"A mate bond?" I questioned sharply, a sharp pang of some unfamiliar emotion going through me. He smiled like he knew what I was feeling, but quickly shook his head no.

"A Pack bond. I've had to break a Pack bond before and it's….hard," he explained and I nodded.

"Hard is one word for it," I commented, touching my forehead. "It's…I feel….lost."

"You never had a Pack," he stated. "The mating bond between us," he paused, searching for the right words, "It became more, it was a Pack bond too."

"It's gone now." The words came out unbearably sad and he closed his eyes, sucking in a sharp breath.

"I didn't want to do it." I nodded, but didn't speak. "I realized I was pulling strength from you. Dangerous amounts. Lethal." He swallowed, his fingers restless. "I couldn't…I couldn't let you die. Not if I could prevent it."

"How did you know I would survive losing the bond?" I questioned, positive there were some who had died from the painful process. I lifted my eyes to his in time to see him smile grimly.

"You are strong. So incredibly strong. Enduring the shift all these years. Living without a Pack? I knew you'd survive if only to come demand answers from me."

"But you didn't know you would be alive to answer them." He shook his head and I sighed, hating my next words but needing to say them anyway. "You can leave now." I unlocked the cage as he blinked at me in surprise. "You broke the bond." I rolled my shoulders. "There's no reason for you to stay now."

He didn't move, his stance stubborn and I lifted my hand. "You can go."

"No."

"Caleb. You have to go. You saw what she did tonight. You think she's going to magically stop?" A mirthless chuckle escaped me. "This was just the beginning. It will only get worse."

"And you know this?"

"I've lived it," I answered without thinking and his eyes hardened. "Trust me, you want to go while you still can. Go be with your Pack. I'm sure they're missing you."

"Not without you."

"Why? There's no bond. You are free."

"What if I don't want to be free?" He contended, moving to the open door, but stopping short of walking out. "What if I want to be with you?"

"I'd think she broke you," I muttered, staring at him like he was crazy. "Tonight should have shown you how incredibly dangerous being with me is. There is no happily ever after here, Caleb." I moved so the door was clear but he stubbornly stayed inside the cell and my head dropped back as I sighed. "She definitely broke you."

"She didn't break me," he promised, taking my hand. "But she did clarify a few things in my head." I tilted my head back down so I could look at him. "I don't want to live without you." I shook my head and he shrugged. "What can I say? I kissed you and I liked it." He tugged on my hand. "This time I want us to know what we're doing. What it means when we give the bite."

"You want us to….to do it again?" I asked in disbelief. "Do the whole mating bond thing again?" I yanked my hand from his and started to pace. "You have definitely lost your marbles, Captain America."

"C'mon, Princess. Isn't there a part of you that feels the same way? I mean you did bite me first."

My mouth opened, but nothing came out as I pointed at him. What he said had some truth but with it came the memory of agonizing loss, a loss that rivaled only my parent's deaths. I wasn't sure I could survive that, not again, and there was zero guarantee it wouldn't happen. If Caleb thought he was saving me, hell, if I thought it would save him, I'd break any bond in a heartbeat, but it would be the last thing I did.

I shook my head, unable to articulate the emotions threatening to choke me, but absolutely not about to put myself through that again.

"Okay, will you think about it?"

"Will you go?" I asked and he shook his head, leaving us at an impasse. My fingers curled around the door of his cage and I swore they bent slightly under the pressure.

"I'm not leaving without you, Princess."

I looked up at him, terrified for us both, and his head came down, slowly enough I could turn away, but I didn't. His lips touched mine, his fingers gentle on my chin as he kissed me thoroughly, each press of his mouth against mine a promise, one I was scared he'd both keep and break. He eased his head back, a bittersweet smile on his face. "That should have been our first kiss."

I chewed on my bottom lip, blurting out the first thing that came to mind. "As long as it's not our last."

He gave me a slow grin, his hand brushing a strand of hair from my face, as he said, "Not by a long shot, Princess."

I shook my head, leaning against the door to push it shut and he stepped back so he was within the cell's perimeter. "If you're not leaving, I guess that means I should lock you up," I uttered, not liking the idea, but he only nodded, seemingly unconcerned at being imprisoned. "She's gonna come back, you know." He nodded again, his eyes glinting like he relished the idea, and I narrowed my own. "What aren't you telling me?"

"Nothing important," he assured me, hands held up innocently. "Trust me. I can handle your grandmother."

An unwilling chuckle swelled in my chest at his statement, but I didn't bother to contradict him. Instead, I slipped my hand through the bars, letting a key dangle from my fingertip. "In case you find out you can't," I offered innocently, the tightness in my chest easing as he accepted the key. "You dying would upset me."

He glanced down at the key in his hand. "Same here, Princess."

Strickland came by to see Gran! The words blasted through my head and from the way Caleb's head jerked, I knew he'd heard them too.

I'm on my way, I told Paige soothingly, stepping away from the bars.

"Why does it matter if Strickland went to see your grandmother?" Caleb questioned, his tone suspicious.

"She was just letting me know," I answered offhandedly, not wanting to tell Caleb that it looked like Strickland might have betrayed us.

"That's not what it sounded like," he replied, his gaze thoughtful. "She sounded scared."

I forced a smile. "Paige freaks out. It's her thing."

"Uh huh." His gaze tracked me as I headed for the stairs. "You can tell me, Dru. All I want is to keep you safe."

"Don't worry," I told him, pausing on the step, my gaze confident. "I've had twenty years of practice doing just that."

***

Oh thank goodness. Paige twisted her fingers together restlessly as my gaze swept the room.

Where is he?

He left, she answered immediately and I glanced at her. *I told him Gran wasn't available.*

Then why the urgent message? I questioned, trying not to grimace since clearly my presence wasn't necessary.

I thought you should know.

My lips compressed, but somehow I managed not to shout. *Has Gran woken up?*

Noooo, Paige drawled in relief. *No sign of her.*

My eyebrows came down but I didn't comment, giving Gran's room a wary glance. There was a saying about letting sleeping bears lie, but I had a feeling that it didn't matter when she woke up, none of us would be safe. *Okay, I'm going to take a quick nap.* I rubbed my gritty eyes, not sure I could sleep even though I was bone tired. Between Paige's energy shot and Caleb's kiss, my body felt like it was buzzing, but I needed sleep if I was going to recover completely. *Wake me if something happens*, I ordered and Paige's head bobbed, her ponytail swinging.

Will do.

I nodded, crawling into the bed gratefully, the sun streaming in through the window not enough to bother me as I closed my eyes. Thoughts swirled like smoke, ephemeral and difficult to pin down, and I gave up trying as my mind shut down, the hours of strain taking their toll.

***

"Why are you still asleep?" The venomous question was accompanied by an abrupt fall as I found myself lying on the floor. I lifted my head to find Gran standing in the doorway, her expression icy with disdain. "I will not allow a lazy lay-about in my home."

There was no point in explaining but I attempted to anyway. "I went hunting last night and didn't return until dawn."

"And you have nothing to show for your hours of *hunting*?" She sneered, making it clear she doubted my explanation. "Strickland returned with two boars. A dangerous hunt, but one that will keep us fed for weeks."

Two weeks at best, I thought to myself, but didn't bother correcting her. "I saw Strickland in the woods," I said instead. "Funny thing, he was not alone."

Gran's eyes widened the tiniest bit and something in my chest squeezed tight.

She'd known.

Strickland's meeting with the hunters – it wasn't at his behest but Gran's. She'd invited hunters onto our land. The only question that remained was why and I knew I would never get a straight answer from her.

Her eyes narrowed to slits and a cold sensation slithered down my spine. "Were you snooping?" She kept her voice low, but it did nothing to disguise the dangerous undercurrent. "Did you follow him, perhaps?" I shook my head slowly, barely breathing as she stepped closer. "Then how did you see Strickland in the woods? *Did he sneak up on you?*" I couldn't answer as power filled the room, sealing out the oxygen with a pop. "Ungrateful child casting accusations, but can't answer a simple question." I struggled to breathe, but it was impossible as she stalked closer. "You've become defiant with the arrival of that *wolf*. Perhaps it's time you were reminded of your place. A place you have only because of my generosity."

I couldn't move as her power arced along my skin, a waterfall compared to the trickle I possessed, and my wolf cowered, unable to defy her command. I wanted to scream in protest, defend myself, but I couldn't get off the ground, my knees glued to the hard floor as she closed in.

Gran, Paige's cheerful voice cut through the ringing in my ears and gave Gran pause. *Where are you? I made your favorite....eggs and oatmeal.* We heard her moving closer and Gran released her power with a snap, causing me to sprawl on the floor in a heap. Paige appeared in the doorway, acting as if she didn't see me on the ground, my forehead touching the cold stone as I sucked in a lungful of air. *I was worried you would be hungry. You missed dinner last night and when I checked on you, you were deep asleep.*

Gran turned, her sour expression lightening as she gazed at Paige. *So thoughtful of you, my dear.* She touched the back of her head, momentary confusion marring her face. *I had quite the headache, but food sounds wonderful.* Paige's gaze strayed to me and Gran moved to block her view. *Unfortunately, Drusilla is on her way out and won't be able to join us…isn't that right?*

Yes, I murmured, keeping my head down as I clenched my fists. *I need to patrol.*

Well, okay. I can save you some if you like?

I forced a smile, glancing up at my sister's sweet face, but I could see the cold rage banked behind her eyes. I would be afraid to eat anything my sister had cooked if I was Gran, but she never seemed to notice. *Not necessary*, I answered, both of us knowing good and well that Gran would throw any leftovers in the trash before she would see me eat them in her current mood. *I'll find something to eat.*

Okay, I promised Sister Margaret I'd visit her today and help with poor Toby.

Gran patted Paige's hand, turning her back to me. *Such a generous and thoughtful child*, she murmured. *Let us go and eat.* Paige shot me a glance, looking deliberately at the wooden dresser before following Gran. I climbed to my feet once they were gone and opened the bottom left drawer. Two hardboiled eggs and another can of Vienna sausage met my eyes and I grinned. I would almost swear Paige could conjure food out of thin air.

I dressed quickly as I shoved the food in my mouth and slipped out the window, not willing to go through the cabin and chance meeting Gran again. She was suspicious, which meant she was twice as dangerous.

Chapter Twelve

Caleb

I'd pocketed the key Dru gave me and the longer I paced, the heavier it felt. Part of me wondered why I just hadn't told her the truth of what I'd done, while another larger part was afraid my actions had achieved nothing, leaving me sitting here defenseless against her Gran. There was no way I'd survive another round with Gran, not without the bond to Dru, and that was a risk I wasn't willing to take until I knew if my blood exchange with her Gran had any effect.

Remembering Gran lying on the floor, defenseless and at my mercy, her words about origins and creation ringing in my ears, I didn't have a single regret about taking her blood. I would have killed her out right if I'd known for sure how it would effect Dru and Paige, and I wasn't talking about their emotional reaction, but what exactly would happen to all that power their Gran was packing. Technically, I still didn't even know what they were, much less how their abilities transferred.

Pack bonds were formed from blood exchanges, usually when the wolf shifter was old enough to understand and consent, but there were plenty of unethical Packs that did blood exchanges with pups, committing them to a Pack without their permission. The fact that I'd done it to their Gran didn't bother me at all. My only concern was whether or not it had worked. I couldn't sense her through any type of normal Pack connection, not like I'd been able to with Dru, but Gran wasn't a wolf, she was something else, something I'd never seen before and honestly kind of hoped I never would have to again.

Her power was dangerous, practically unchecked, and she made no bones about hating wolves. If it hadn't been for Paige, I would be dead, a fact I didn't take lightly, but I wasn't leaving without Dru. I'd broken our bond, and I was pretty sure I'd splintered my soul in the process, but an agonizing death had a way of clarifying things. Dru was my mate, my only mate, and I would do anything to keep her safe, to show her how much I loved and needed her. I wasn't leaving until we recreated the bond and became one.

Caleb! The panicky shout echoed in my head as Paige's face appeared above me, staring down through the bars that made up the ceiling. Her wide eyes were terrified and my heart stopped, knowing she would only be that scared if something had happened to….

Dru? I questioned, ready to leap up and rip the bars apart if necessary. Paige shook her head then nodded, and I scowled. *Is Dru alright?* I enunciated slowly, intensely regretting the loss of our bond and my ability to just touch her mind. *Answer me*, I roared as Paige just stared.

She's okay, Paige replied, jumping at my yell. My sudden relief was ruined by her next words though. *But there's an army.*

I squinted, trying to process her words. *An army?*

She nodded frantically, pointing to the south. *Dru spotted them while patrolling. They haven't come onto our land, but there are so many of them. I think they're going to kill her.*

I blinked, then focused on the Pack bond I shared with Dom and the rest of the Navarre Pack. They were close, extremely close, and I knew one word would from me would bring them charging over the border and onto Ghost Pack land. Only Pack law kept Dom in check but I had to go and defuse the situation before he decided my life was worth a war.

I need to get out, I told Paige and she nodded, standing up. I dug in my pocket, flashing the key at her. *I got it.* She looked surprised but didn't comment. *Is the coast clear?*

She glanced around, carefully sweeping the area. *Yes*, she reported. *I'll meet you at the stairs.*

I unlocked the door, wondering if Dru had any idea I'd be using the key so soon. I jogged up the steps, my calf muscles cramping at the exercise. It had only been a few days, but after what Gran had put me through it felt more like months of captivity. *Can you guide me to them?* I asked Paige and she nodded, taking the lead. *Without winding up in a trap?* I added, and she gave me an annoyed frown. *Just checking*, I muttered, careful to watch where she placed her feet.

Paige didn't speak but I could feel the emotion radiating from her. It came in pulsating waves and I wasn't sure she even realized she was doing it. Fear was the predominant emotion, but there was also a cold rage that had me following close on her heels, afraid of what she might do if she thought her sister was threatened.

They won't hurt her, I attempted to reassure Paige, but not feeling at all reassured by her reply.

They better not.

It took us the better part of an hour to reach the southern border, and I was sure the only reason Dom hadn't crossed the border was because he felt me coming closer. The Pack bond vibrated the closer we came, each link a vibrant connection to my Pack mates, but none of them came close to the one I shared with Dom. He'd been the one to initiate me into the Pack, the one to bring me back from the brink of death, and the one who never gave up on me.

"Dom."

His gaze swung to me, piercing yellow eyes pinning me in place as he assured himself that I was in fact okay. "Every. Single. Day." My lips twitched and he shook his head. "Was that too much to ask for?"

I shrugged and padded closer, knowing his sharp gaze hadn't missed the fact that I wasn't in peak condition. "I lost my phone?"

Lips pressed together as he eyed me. "You weren't where you said you were."

I tilted my head in acknowledgement. "No, but you never wanted me here."

"For good reason," he retorted, his eyes skipping behind me. I didn't need to turn to know that Dru had stepped up behind me. "Who are you?"

"Dru." We replied in unison and he closed his eyes briefly, pinching the bridge of his nose.

"God help me."

"We have bigger problems," I said, right before the scent of ozone met my nose and I could see Dom's nose crinkle. "Yeah. That."

"What is that?"

"You dare to invade my land?" Gran's voice cracked like a whip and Paige cowered slightly behind her sister. "How dare you come here?"

"Technically, we're on our land, not yours," a familiar voice piped up as Jess stepped around Dom, his enormous bulk hiding her completely, and we could all see Gran was taken aback by her presence. "And why exactly are you keeping a member of *our* Pack prisoner?" She crossed her arms over her chest, either unable to feel the power pulsing from Gran or just not caring. It was really hard to tell with Jess.

"I'm Dominic Navarre, Alpha of the Navarre Pack, and Caleb is mine," Dom bit out, looking pissed. "Who are you?"

"Watch your tone, pup," Gran snarled, sweeping closer and I could see Dom's chest swell slightly. He wasn't the only one though as Trent, Liam, and Monster all tensed. Paige hadn't been exaggerating when she'd said there was an army. Over a dozen shifters stood at the edge of the forest, a mix of members from both Dom and Anna's Packs, ready to do whatever it took to bring me home. My gaze skimmed the varying shifters, some young, others older, all capable of fighting, but I paused as I came to

Dylan. I was surprised to see him since he didn't care for me at all with good reason. I hadn't exactly welcomed him to my Pack with open arms all those years ago, a fact I wasn't proud of.

A Down syndrome wolf shifter was dangerous, unpredictable, and often uncontrollable. While they didn't intend to hurt anyone their emotions could often get the better of them. Dylan was no different, but he was fiercely loyal to one wolf shifter in particular, following him wherever he went. My gaze strayed to Monster, or Theo Carter, brother to Jess Carter, who was mated to Dom, my Alpha. Where Monster went, Dylan followed, no exception. I guess I shouldn't be surprised then that he was here. The only one who had been as interested in the Ghost Pack as me was Monster and I could see his avid gaze taking in every nuance of the confrontation.

Static electricity filled the air and I tensed, ready for whatever she was about to dish out, when another voice spoke, "Don't think about using your tricks, Mildred. I would hate to know you'd fallen so far as to break our laws." The electricity fizzled instantly and Gregory stepped out from the forest, a cane in his hand. "It's been a long time, Millie."

"Do not call me by that ridiculous nickname," she commanded, not an ounce of her inherent regality diminished by his reprimand. "And not nearly long enough, Gregory."

Gregory shook his head. "What are you doing, Mildred?" The oldest member of our combined Packs had a disappointed expression, one that would leave any young shifter quaking, but *Millie* only narrowed her eyes at him. "Kidnapping a Pack wolf? Threatening to use your power against an allied Pack?"

"Allied?" I burst out, turning to stare at him as Dru turned an accusing gaze on Gran. "No one said anything about an alliance with the Ghost Pack."

"I don't recall anyone asking," Gregory chided gently and I lowered my head in acknowledgement.

"Wait a damn second," Trent interrupted, holding up his hand. "I've been here before and wasn't exactly welcomed."

Gran gave him a cold stare, stating, "You have never been here."

Trent opened his mouth, ready to argue no doubt, but when I saw the frantic beat of Dru's pulse, I shook my head, and he swallowed whatever he was about to say. "Sorry, I must have confused you with some other Ghost Pack."

Dom's eyes flickered to mine, ***What*** *exactly has been going on here?*

Later, I promised over the Pack link I shared with him.

"Your *wolf* came onto our land without permission. Detaining him was well within my rights." Gran or Mildred – Millie just didn't fit the stern woman facing down multiple shifters – flicked her fingers. "As for any alliance there may have been….that died with your previous Alpha." My stomach clenched knowing she referred to my father, and his death over a decade before. Dru glanced at me, the sympathy in her eyes telling me she must have known some of the story.

Gran made a show of looking around. "I also don't see your Alpha here. Why is that? Scared?" She taunted, letting her eyes glow slightly.

Trent bristled, stepping forward to defend his absent wife, but Dom moved in front of him. "No. We have no reason to fear you," he commented and we all felt the snap in the air as she recognized his insult. "It seems you have an issue with wolf shifters."

"Putting it mildly," I muttered, but with all of the sensitive ears surrounding me, no one missed it. Except....

What's going on? Paige demanded, frustration lacing her voice as her gaze bounced around the gathering. *I can't keep up.*

Apparently, our elder knew your Gran back in the day, I reported. *He called her Millie.*

Millie!?! Paige screeched disbelievingly, causing me and Dru to wince, but I also noticed Monster's head jerk, almost like he'd heard her too.

Gran's been holding out on us, Dru added, her voice dangerous.

"Your kind isn't welcome here," Gran snapped, flipping her hand toward me. "Take your foolish pup and go." Her eyes glittered with warning. "And consider yourselves lucky I let you live."

"What happened, Mildred?" Gregory said heavily, the deep folds on his face one of the only signs of his 130 years on this earth. "We used to be friends."

"Ages ago. Things change," Mildred replied crisply, but it was the first time I'd seen even a hint of softness on her face. "I don't blame you," she added cryptically and I exchanged a glance with Dru. "But I also won't allow your kind to harm another of my children."

A frown marred Gregory's face. "Our kind? Have you forgotten where we came from?"

Gran's expression iced over and I could swear the air temperature dropped. "I have not. But perhaps you should teach your children their origins." Her gaze pinned me in place. "Then they'll know to respect their betters."

"Betters?" I echoed, taking a stride in her direction before Dru's hand settled on my arm, halting me. "You're no better than a Hanley," I sneered, unable to think of a worse insult. Power slammed into me, shoving me back which caused Dru's hand to fall, and my fist clenched in anger as I felt Gran's intention.

No, I gritted, pushing back and this time she staggered in shock. Dom hovered, his gaze bouncing as he sensed something happening, but couldn't figure out what.

Did....did you just defy her? Paige asked with a mixture of awe and terror.

My chest rose and fell as I kept my gaze locked on Mildred, daring her to try again. A glint entered her eyes and I prepared myself as the ground trembled beneath us.

"Enough," Dru shouted, stepping between us. "Enough. You've done enough, Gran. Let him go." She panted and I realized Mildred had switched her focus to Dru. Paige stepped forward then, her hand slipping into Dru's to create a united front.

Who is she? Dom and Monster's voices echoed in unison, catching sight of Paige for the first time.

"Your defiance wears thin," Gran warned, pointing at Dru, then glanced at Paige, her nose scrunching. "You think you are helping your sister?" The words echoed eerily in my head and I realized she spoke them verbally and mentally.

Paige's breath hitched but she didn't back down. *She's my sister. I won't let you hurt her. Not anymore.*

Gran looked taken aback and I took advantage, placing my hand on Dru's shoulder. "I'll leave, but she comes with me."

"No." There was no hesitation in the denial, but it didn't come from Mildred. My hand slipped from Dru as she turned to me, her expression apologetic. "I already told you I won't leave."

"She'll kill you," I objected hoarsely and Dru shook her head.

"She hasn't yet."

Tell me what's going on, Paige demanded, watching us.

"You hear that?" Monster questioned, glancing around in puzzlement, and confirming to me that he actually could hear Paige. "Who is that?" Dom shot him a concerned glance, clearly not hearing her, but I didn't have time to reassure him that Monster wasn't crazy. It seemed I could hear Dru when she and Paige were conversing, even with the mate bond broken.

Your sister won't come with me. I couldn't keep the hurt out of my voice and Dru flinched. *She's determined to stay.*

Because of me, Paige determined.

Not just you, Dru argued, but it fell flat.

Paige pushed her sister, who stumbled back, looking surprised as Paige shoved her again. *What are you doing?* Dru demanded, digging her feet in as Paige continued to try and move her closer to the border of our lands. *Paige*, she said sharply.

"GO." The single word was loud and garbled, but recognizable.

"I heard that," Dom said to no one in particular as Dru and I stared at Paige in shock.

"Go," she repeated, stretching out the word as her lips formed the unfamiliar shape. "Go."

"No," Dru said, shaking her head, then repeating over their link, *No*.

"Yessss," Paige responded and I blinked at the sharpness of the single word. Her tone was off, but there was no mistaking what she was saying. Paige's face was full of frustration though as she blasted us with her thoughts. *You don't get to stay for me. Go and run. Be free, sister.*

I can't, Dru replied, her eyes glossy. *Leaving you –* She shook her head. *You know what that means.*

Gran gripped Dru's arm tight enough to make her wince as she growled, "If you leave you'll never be welcome back here." She shook Dru hard enough to make her head bob. "I will make sure you never see your sister again," she hissed, her voice dropping so low I had to strain to hear it. "I will make sure she doesn't see the light of day."

Dru ripped out of Gran's hold, her eyes catching mine for the barest moment, but it was long enough for me to see bitter regret reflected in them. I dropped the hand I was stretching toward her. "Go with them," she whispered, the words broken and desperate. *Don't let her hurt them*, she told Paige, whose face fell as Dru rejected her plea for her to be free.

Dru leapt, her body contorting in the air and she landed on four paws, her fur the color of straw. I grabbed Paige when she collapsed against me as Dru disappeared into the woods. *Gran threatened to hurt you*, I murmured, squeezing Paige gently. *Dru won't leave because she thinks she's protecting you.*

I always knew Gran...didn't treat Dru right, but I never thought she used me against her. A whimper escaped her and I supported her weight, staring at the spot where Dru had vanished. *She can't do this.* With Paige's words a veil dropped over any hint of her emotions and their absence was more chilling than her rage.

A hard stare drew my attention and I saw Monster watching us closely, his gaze tracking where my arm braced Paige. I carefully withdrew my arm, making sure she was steady, but she didn't seem to notice, her attention fully focused on Gran. *Easy, kid. Don't burn the forest down for one rotten tree.* Her expression smoothed as she gave me a short nod.

Your safety is my responsibility and I won't fail you, she said formally and a quick frown flashed across my face. *But you have to go.* I started to shake my head when her eyes flashed neon blue, bright enough to sear me. *This isn't negotiable. Dru won't come back until you're gone.* She hesitated, her voice barely a whisper as she added, *I can't fight Gran on my own.*

Everything inside me wanted to protest, to tell her my leaving wasn't negotiable, that I was here for Dru no matter what, but the memory of Dru's face wouldn't leave me. Gran had forced her into an untenable choice, one I couldn't in good conscious make harder on her. Leaving went against my instincts, but I knew Paige was right. Dru was stubborn but conceding now didn't mean I was giving up.

I'm coming back, I warned her and she bit her lip.

I'm counting on it, she replied, stepping away from me.

The wind started to whip and without warning I was blasted off my feet. I flew backwards, not stopping until I hit a tree, and squinted against the swirling leaves to see Gran, her eyes burning as she held out her hand. "This is your only warning. Stay away from here. You are not welcome."

"Millie," Gregory shouted and something flashed across her face before her expression shuttered and he skidded backwards, coming to a stop once he was back on our Pack lands. "It doesn't have to be this way," he tried again, his expression pained.

She didn't answer, turning her back to us in a clear dismissal. Dom paced the line, a snarl escaping him at her insult, but he checked himself as I came up beside him. "Leave it, brother." I rested my hand on his shoulder, pressing him back, not able to watch Gran and Paige walk away. "Another day."

He shot me a sharp glance, repeating, "Another day?"

I nodded, unable to stop myself as I glanced over my shoulder, but they were already gone. "She's my mate."

He sighed heavily, but didn't argue, just clamped a hand on my shoulder. "I'm glad you're okay." He shook his head. "Scared the hell out of me when I felt you –" he stopped, choking up and shoved me. "Don't do that again."

I nodded, not making any promises, my gaze lingering where Dru had disappeared. "I'll be back," I vowed, only walking away when Trent nudged me.

"Come on, troublemaker." I glanced at him, a smile almost but not quite forming when he added, "Dom practically skinned me alive when I admitted where you were."

"You told him?" I asked in disbelief. Trent wasn't exactly the type to go out on a limb for me.

"You died. You do realize that?"

I grunted, elbowing him. "Yeah, I was there."

Trent chuckled mirthlessly. "You still don't get it, do you?" I glanced at him, surprised at the bitterness in his question. "He worries about you as much if not more than his own kids. I was there when he felt your Pack link disappear, knowing exactly what that meant. You're the reason he has gray hair."

"I wasn't trying…"

Trent interrupted, "I know that, he knows that, but damn it, Caleb, for once think about someone other than yourself." He stopped, yanking me around. "There are people that care about you, love you, who would die for you." He gestured to the Ghost Pack land. "Proof enough today. The least you could do is acknowledge it."

I reared back at the accusation in his voice. "I didn't ask –"

"Stop. Just stop right there." He shook his head, walking off and leaving me standing there.

An arm hooked around mine, linking us together, and I didn't bother to glance down, knowing who had joined me. "Am I really a petulant brat?"

Jess sighed, cocking her head as she watched Trent stomp off. "No. Not anymore. You can't be responsible for how other people react, Caleb. You can only be responsible for your own actions."

"And coming here was irresponsible," I concluded and she grimaced. "Go ahead, yell at me."

"No." I glanced down at her in surprise. "You didn't do anything wrong, Caleb. It's your life and you're a grown man who has to make his own way." She smiled ruefully. "Dom just isn't very good at letting go." She shook her head, her forehead wrinkling. "I'm not relishing when the kids leave the nest. I'm pretty sure he's gonna want to build tiny houses for them in the backyard." I snorted, but didn't deny her words. It sounded like Dom. "He knows, you know." Her voice tightened as she squeezed my arm and I sucked in a harsh breath. "He understands why you don't come back. He doesn't blame you, but he does miss you." Her eyes were damp as she looked at me, forcing a smile. "Welcome home, Caleb." She slipped away, her stride lengthening as she joined Dom, and I watched him adjust his stride to match hers, linking their hands together.

A deep stab of longing hit me, made worse by the fact that now I knew exactly what it felt like to have that sense of connection with my own mate. My steps slowed, the urge to go back strong, but I resisted, needing to respect Dru and Paige's wishes, at least for now. A cane swept the ground in front of me, halting my steps. "We need to talk," Gregory declared and I nodded shortly.

"We do," I agreed, giving him a sideways glance. "Seems there's a few things about our history that have been left out of the books."

Gregory's mouth tightened as he shook his head. "I never agreed with your father's ruling on that, but he wasn't one you challenged and lived to tell about it." My jaw locked at the reminder of the iron fist my father had wielded over the Pack. He'd always had a reason, but rarely bothered to share it. "Don't," he exhaled, shaking his head. "Don't underestimate them."

An unwilling laugh barked out of me. "She killed me, Gregory. Trust me, I know exactly how powerful they are." Every one of Gregory's years showed as his gaze turned inward. "You knew her. Was she always like this?"

"Our acquaintance was many, *many* years ago." He sighed. "A lot can happen in the long span of our lives." His mouth turned down. "People change and as we grow older we make compromises that as youth we never thought we would."

"Another question," I paused, waiting for his consent.

He smiled, "I think I owe you a few questions, young Caleb."

"How similar are they to us?"

His smile disappeared. "Never assume they are like us, Caleb. They're not. They have abilities we will never have," he paused, his voice heavy, "And apparently a strong disdain for our kind."

"A well-earned one," I admitted, scratching my jaw, the golden bristle itchy after several days without shaving. "Dru told me some of their history. Gran," I paused and corrected myself, "Mildred was betrayed by her husband and Hanleys killed her daughter. I can't blame her for her hatred."

"If only she'd reached out to our Pack, as allies we would have assisted her."

"Would our Pack have assisted her?" I questioned and Gregory gave me a startled glance. "Father wanted to erase the history of our origins. Perhaps he also wanted to erase those responsible."

"That's a strong accusation, Caleb," Gregory replied cautiously and I laughed bitterly.

"He's dead, Gregory. He can't haunt me anymore." I glanced over at him. "But you know it's possible."

Gregory dipped his head in acknowledgement. "With your father, anything was possible."

"Blood exchange is important to Packs. Is it equally important to them?" I referred to Gran and her granddaughters as *them*, simply because I didn't have a name, at least not one I wanted to use because it seemed so impossible to my mind – my apparently ignorant mind I was beginning to learn.

"They place a great deal of importance on their blood, yes, but do they use it like we do? That I don't know." Gregory gave me a rueful smile. "Millie was always secretive when it came to her power." He tilted his head. "Not without good reason it would seem." He clapped his hand on my shoulder. "Enough for now. We'll continue this once we're home." His stare turned contemplative. "It's time I told the story of how wolf shifters came to be."

Chapter Thirteen

Dru

I ran, the pain of the shift no match for the pain in my heart after telling him no, and seeing Paige's desperation for me to be free. I hadn't realized how strongly she'd felt until I'd heard her voice, the effort she'd made to speak, but I also couldn't allow her to carry the burden of our grandmother's hatred alone.

One of my paws glanced off metal and I heard the snap as the metal teeth locked together. I skidded to a stop, heart pounding at how close I'd come to being caught in one of our own traps. I sat down on my haunches, staring at the rusted jaws, desperate to know what was happening in the clearing between Gran and the dozen shifters that had come for Caleb, but also afraid I wouldn't be strong enough to tell him no again if he asked.

I'd been surprised when I'd come across the shifters pacing along the border and the lone woman among them. Fear had been my first emotion, followed by relief that maybe Caleb would actually be safe if they'd come to free him. Gran would hesitate to try and attack so many, especially if she didn't have Paige by her side.

Once I'd assured myself that the scent of the wolf shifters was in fact the same as Caleb, I'd sent a frantic message to Paige, knowing she'd bring Caleb to me. Gran's arrival had been unexpected even though I should have known better. Her arrival had thrown gasoline on a tense situation, but it was the old wolf who'd surprised me. He'd known her, called her by a nickname, and Gran hadn't killed him instantly for it.

Finding out we'd once been allies with Caleb's Pack had been a punch to the gut. Gran had kept so much from us in her effort to ostracize and control us. Maybe if we'd asked for help all those years ago, my grandmother and mother wouldn't have died and Gran wouldn't be the acrimonious old woman she was now.

I stared back the way I'd come, broken branches indicating my rush as I'd torn though the forest. A low whine escaped me as I stood and paced. My wolf wanted to go back, recognizing her mate was out there and not understanding why we weren't fighting for him.

She'll never see daylight again, the hissed words drifted through my mind once again and I closed my eyes, knowing Gran would do it. She'd cage Paige up like an animal and leave her there to die just to spite me. I'd never been one to toe the line, but once Gran had figured out the one thing I loved more than myself, she'd had me. I would do anything for Paige, a fact Gran was well aware of and it had cost me dearly, but I couldn't bring myself to regret Paige's existence. I would have broken long ago if it hadn't been for her.

I chuffed, shaking my head, not able to sense Paige's emotions any longer. A few steps forward and I paused, wolf and human warring over the best course of action. Finally, we settled on watch and wait, my steps eager now as I trotted back to the clearing. It didn't take me long to reach them, but already they were disappearing, the wolf shifters going back home. Only one concerned me though and I watched him hesitate, his gaze sweeping right over where I hid and I tucked myself further back, afraid he could somehow see me.

"I'll be back," the low whisper should have been impossible to hear, but there was no mistaking Caleb's voice. He turned and in a few strides was gone.

My breath left me in a rush as I tried to decipher the tangle of emotions his leaving caused, there was relief, but also a bone crushing sorrow at watching another person I loved leave me. I rubbed my snout against my paw, the ache in my chest spreading the longer he was gone until it felt like it would consume me.

Dru? Paige's voice nudged me, reminding me I wasn't alone, and I struggled to lift my head. *Dru,* she hesitated, her voice full of apology. *I'm sorry I didn't know.*

It's okay, I murmured, exhaustion tugging at me, but it wasn't the kind that you could fix with enough sleep. It went deeper and I was afraid I'd never escape it. *You're alright?*

There was a long pause before she finally answered with a *Yeah,* which neither of us believed. Everything had changed and there was no going back to the way it was before Caleb had crashed into our lives. We had to break the stranglehold Gran held over us and the few left in our tiny village. We needed to stop letting our lives drift by us.

Are you ready? I asked Paige. *It won't be easy*, I warned, knowing Gran would fight us tooth and nail.

Seeing them....A Pack like that, I wanted you to be free, to go with them, Paige answered, the words desperate. *But you couldn't go. You couldn't be free because I'm not free.*

It's not your fault, I hastened to reassure her, feeling her pang of guilt. *You can't control how our power is inherited or our mother's choices.*

I could leave, she said simply and my mouth twisted into a grimace. *I could. I should*, she continued insistently. *It's my own selfishness that keeps me here. And forces you to remain.*

And your continued desire to live, I countered. *You would die if you left,* I reminded her harshly. *Your power would fade and with it your life.*

Eventually, she responded, determination in her voice.

Quickly, I warned, adding firmly, *It's not an option.*

It's not your decision to make, she protested and an unhappy laugh escaped me at her tone. *It's not, Dru. Why won't you let me make this choice for you?*

Because I know, I cried out, silencing her. *I know how fast your power fades. I know exactly how many minutes it takes for you to gasp for air. I know because Gran did it when you were a baby to show me.*

The truth hung in the air between us, fragile as a bubble, a lifetime of secrets weaved between us, each trying to save the other.

Why didn't you tell me?

Because I love you, I replied, the air shimmering around me as I shifted, welcoming the agony as my bones twisted and cracked, each tendon stretching until it couldn't anymore, finally snapping and shredding as my body contorted back into human form.

"About time you showed back up," Gran snapped, appearing in front of me, silent as a ghost. "Running off like a lovesick child. I thought better of you."

"Did you?" I inquired sweetly, walking past her.

"Don't walk away from me," she ordered and I twisted around, lifting my hands in surrender.

"Ooooh, no, what are you going to do to me? Kill me?" I gasped, fluttering my eyelashes. "Finally. What a relief. I thought you were just going to toy with me again."

"You think you can talk back to me?" Her voice lowered dangerously and my heart skipped. I was taunting the beast knowingly. If anyone was aware of what she could do, it was me, so why was I basically asking for her to punish me?

"I don't know if you still have it, Gran." My shoulders rose and dropped. "You couldn't control Caleb." It was a risky move, one I instantly regretted when she jerked my feet out from under me, her power pressing me into facedown into the ground. I tried to resist, pushing against the blanket of power, but it was no use. I couldn't fight her, which made me question how Caleb had managed it. We'd all felt the pulse of power she'd sent at him, but he'd somehow managed to defy her. I'd thought maybe I could do the same, but as I flopped like a fish on the ground I knew I'd been wrong.

Stop! Paige's feet appeared in front of me as she stood between Gran and me.

Don't, I tried to warn her, but she didn't listen.

Stop hurting Dru! Her foot stomped and I almost smiled. *She's done nothing to deserve this. Neither of us have. Why do you hate us?* She wailed and the power holding me abruptly disappeared.

Hate? You think I hate you? I crawled to my knees, swaying as I looked around Paige's knees to see Gran. Her lips pinched together, her expression formidable as always, but there was a glimmer in her eyes that hinted at hurt. *Some would say I hated your mother, that I allowed her weakness to define her....destroy her.* I sucked in a sharp breath at her mention of our mother. It wasn't often Gran talked about her so we both listened intently. *I vowed I wouldn't allow that to happen to the two of you. I wouldn't make the same mistakes. I coddled your mother, allowed her to follow her heart, and look what happened.*

Gran raised her chin and I slowly got to my feet. I had been old enough to see the devotion between my parents, a devotion that had excluded anyone else – including me and Paige. She'd been lost after his death, a shadow without an anchor, and even more absent than normal. I wish I could say I missed her, but it had never felt like I'd had her. Dad was the one who'd given us his time and attention. It was his death that had been the blow, forever altering all of our lives.

I didn't want the same thing to happen to you, she stated unapologetically.

So you tortured Dru? Paige accused, waving her hand. *You keep us prisoner? Use us against one another?*

The world is an unforgiving place, one that has no care for the weak. I won't allow it to do the same to you.

"You just thought you'd break me yourself," I muttered under my breath and she cast a sharp glance at me.

"I saved you," she replied tautly. "A dozen times before your first birthday." I stilled as she swallowed. "People reject those that are different. Their cruelty knows no bounds."

"I....I didn't know," I stammered.

"Nor should you have," she said crisply. *"Let's go home,"* her voice echoed in my head and ears, bringing the conversation back to Paige.

We exchanged a glance. *That's it?* I couldn't disguise my shock, positive Gran had some terrible punishment planned for us.

Her mouth formed a moue of displeasure, her gaze flickering to the forest where Caleb and the others had gone. *I hear there's a lovely boar for us to enjoy. No sense in it going to waste.* She spun on her heel and marched back toward home, leaving Paige and I to trail behind her, baffled by this new side of Gran.

The walk home was long, Gran unerringly stepping over every single trap, but I found myself glancing over my shoulder every few steps. The further we got from the border the more my feet dragged. The urge to go back intensified and I faltered. Paige's hand slipped into mine, squeezing gently. *He'll come back,* she assured me and the churning in my stomach worsened.

That's what I'm afraid of, I replied tartly, straightening my back. *He's going to get himself killed.*

I don't know, Paige mused. *He seems to have more lives than a cat.*

I snorted, amused in spite of myself. *He is unnaturally lucky.*

He must be since he won your heart, Paige chortled, dashing away when I swiped at her.

A few minutes later, we entered the village to find everyone gathered around a spit. The smell of roasting meat filled the air and my mouth watered. Greetings filled the air when they saw Gran, several bobbing their heads toward her. She smiled, the queen amongst her subjects as they parted, eager to have her in their midst. Paige followed in her wake receiving welcoming smiles that quickly faded as I brought up the rear.

Plates appeared piled high with succulent meat which Gran accepted graciously, passing one to each of us as the villagers gave me a wide berth. I used my fingers to stuff several bites in my mouth, the meat burning my tongue, but too starved to slow down.

Gran sighed impatiently when she caught sight of me and Paige hid a grin, daintily using a knife and fork. Awkward silence fell over the clearing, several casting wary glances toward me. I paused mid-bite, the meat falling from my fingertips as my appetite disappeared.

Ignore them, Paige pleaded, covering my hand with hers. *Stay and they'll get used to you.*

I looked up, the sky above blurring for a second. *I doubt that*, I commented, striving for a light tone, but falling flat. *It's been thirty years. I don't think one more meal is going to change anyone's mind.* I stood up, the motion too fast to be human, and one of the women skittered backwards, the plate in her hand falling to the ground. Everyone stared at me and Paige pressed her lips together, regret shining in her eyes as I slowly backed away. *I'll be at home*, I told her and she nodded, this time not bothering to stop me. I took the plate with me, finishing it off before I'd reached the house.

I dumped the empty dish in the sink and stood there, staring at the wall blankly. Again, I asked myself if I was doing the right thing by staying in a place where everyone feared me. Did I really think Gran would make Paige suffer for my absence?

This morning, I would have unequivocally said yes, but now I wasn't so sure. Today, a crack had appeared in the shell Gran had maintained for most of my life, and I was starting to realize my existence was more complicated than I'd ever imagined.

I pressed the heel of my palm against my eyes, cursing their differences and my inability to do anything about it. I lowered my hands, grime coating my fingertips as I rubbed them together, and sighed. I debated heating water for a bath, but decided it would take too long. A cold shower would be sufficient for me, but I went ahead and filled the tub, starting a fire underneath so the water would be hot when Paige came home.

I set the shower to a trickle as I scrubbed my skin roughly, working under my fingernails and toenails, and combing the soap through my hair. My skin pebbled in the cold air, but I didn't stop until every inch of me was clean. I turned up the water, letting the ice cold water drench me, the filthy water swirling down the drain under my feet. My toes curled but I stood under the water until it ran clear. The rusty knob screeched as I twisted it off and I grabbed a worn towel to dry myself. The rough cotton scratched my skin, turning it red as I vigorously rubbed it all over me, warming myself.

A simple, white shift hung on a hook, and I pulled it over my head and padded into the small room I shared with Paige. A low fire burned so I added a few logs, stirring until the flames licked higher, warming the room. I crawled into my bed, tugging an old quilt over me as I settled into the lumpy mattress. Sleep eluded me though as the memory of the wolf shifters refused to leave me.

I knew they'd come for Caleb and he was safe with them, but I hadn't expected the deep yearning I'd feel to go with them. My wolf had whined, recognizing her kind, and it had taken every ounce of my strength not to shift and join them. She wanted to prance, play, and run with a pack, a longing I thought I'd buried so deep it was gone, but seeing them had proven me wrong.

I rubbed my face against the threadbare sheet, pressing until I had to lift my head and gasp for air, but it did nothing to curb the need to run. I curled myself into a ball, forcing myself to stay still as I stared at the unadorned log walls, each breath slower than the last as I counted each crack, all eight hundred and ninety-two of them.

***

Something jolted me awake and I lifted my head, thinking Paige coming in had woken me, but when I glanced at her bed, I could see her sleeping peacefully, and the fire had died down to ember. I scooted out of the bed, surprised she'd come in without waking me, and went to the fireplace, wondering what had woken me. I added another log to the fire so it wouldn't go out and seeing only a couple logs left, decided to go get more. I glanced at the door, but didn't want to risk waking Gran so I went to the window instead, easing the sash open and slipping outside.

I hurried to the stack of wood, but a light at the back door gave me pause. I slipped closer and was startled to hear raised voices. I ducked out of sight as Strickland came to the door, his expression angry and, I narrowed my eyes as I realized, *nervous*. *What would cause Strickland to be nervous*, I wondered, *and who was he arguing with?*

Gran's stern face appeared behind him and I ducked closer to the wall, afraid she might see me spying. "I'll deal with it," she stated with finality, but Strickland's face turned mutinous.

"You let him go," he accused and Gran's mouth flattened. "What am I supposed to do? They want what they paid for."

"You will do nothing. I have *already* said I'll handle it," she said sharply, her tone brooking no argument. He opened his mouth, ready to protest, and she snapped her fingers in front of his lips, sealing them shut. "We are done." His eyes widened as he struggled to pry his lips apart, but it was no use, I knew. She'd done it to me a dozen times and until the magic wore off, his lips were literally sealed. He sucked air in through his nose, his eyes burning and she wiggled her fingers in a shooing motion. "Don't make me force your obedience," she warned, while looking entirely too delighted by the prospect. He stumbled backwards, an expression of dawning horror as he experienced firsthand what Gran was capable of when thwarted. I *almost* felt bad for him, but he'd been one to make my life miserable every chance he got, plus he'd been consorting with hunters.

I waited until the light was off and Strickland had disappeared far enough into the darkness even my keen eyesight couldn't spot him, before I gathered an armful of wood and went back to the room. I laid the logs down carefully, not worried about disturbing Paige, but I wanted no reason for Gran to question if

I'd potentially overheard her conversation with Strickland.

What took you so long? My hand jerked at the loud question, and one of the logs slipped out of my grip, thumping loudly, and causing me to freeze and glance at the door. *Sorry, I didn't mean to startle you*, Paige whispered unnecessarily in my head and I chuckled softly. I gently finished laying down the wood and turned to her.

It's fine, I murmured, taking in her wide blue eyes peering up at me from the bed. *I was just getting more wood for the fire.*

You were gone a long time.

I smirked at her, tucking my feet under the quilt to warm them. *Keeping tabs on me now?*

She lowered her eyelashes, hiding her eyes from me as she said softly, *I thought you might not come back.*

My breath gusted out of as if I'd been sucker punched. *Paige.*

I wouldn't blame you if you did, she rushed to say, her fingers twisting the quilt under her hands. *I saw it, you know, the way you looked at them.* I crawled out of my bed and went to hers, nudging her so she'd let me slide in next to her. She scooted over, still not looking at me.

I won't lie. It was more tempting than I realized, I admitted, the words coming out easier under the cloak of darkness. *But it still wasn't enough to make me leave you.* Her head nestled next to mine as our fingers wove together, the position a familiar one since we'd done it a thousand times growing up. *I wish there was an easy answer, Paige, but life....it doesn't work that way.*

Then why do all the stories end with happily ever after?

Because, I paused, exhaling as I tried to find the right words, *because happiness is a choice...one that belongs to each of us.* The words came out haltingly, but I knew they were true. *We make our own happiness. We can't depend on others to do it for us. We make our choices and we live with them.*

But what if others dictate our choice? Paige argued and I turned my head, kissing her forehead as I told her a hard truth.

Because it's still our choice even if we don't like the options.

Like staying.

No, not like staying, I denied, stroking her hair. *Staying....I'll never regret staying with you, little sister.*

She didn't comment, snuggling against me. *Sleep here?* She asked, squeezing my hand like she had a thousand times before and I nodded, no longer sleepy, but content to lay there with her until she fell asleep.

Thoughts chased themselves in a never ending loop as I tried to decipher the conversation I'd overheard. I knew it must have something to do with the hunters, but my mind shied away from the implications. Logic would tell me they'd intended to sell Caleb to the hunters, but why? Why would she do that? What purpose would it serve?

Memories of other shifters she had tortured over the years drifted through my mind. I'd always assumed they'd died, but what if she'd sold them as well? And if she had, why hadn't she done it to me?

A soft snore escaped Paige and I eased my arm out from under her, careful not to disturb her. She might not be able to hear, but all her other senses made up for the lack. I carefully got dressed, shoving my feet into a pair of too tight boots, and wiggled my toes uncomfortably. I wasn't used to wearing shoes, but tonight I wasn't running, I was hunting and I wanted to make damn sure they heard me coming.

***

My first stop left me frustrated when I didn't find him, and my plodding pace in the boots irritated me until I finally yanked them off and left them at the edge of the forest. Once my toes were free to dig into the soft earth, I could breathe again. It only took a few deep breaths to pick up his trail and I stalked him to a clearing where he was talking on a phone.

I cocked my head, surprised, since I'd thought only Gran kept a phone. "Full of secrets, aren't you, Strickland?" I murmured, watching him intently.

"Don't worry. I have it. I just need time." He paused, listening to whoever spoke and through I strained I couldn't pick up on the other person's words. "Trust me, this is better."

His heart beat faster than normal and the sickly scent of nerves filled the air as he defied Gran and betrayed all of us. My fingers curled into my palms as my nails lengthened, growing sharp and deadly and as he ended the call, I crept up behind him.

He froze as a single nail settled on his jugular, the slightest pressure enough to send it piercing through his skin and ending his life. "Whatcha doing, Strickland?" I whispered in his ear then watched as a bead of sweat trickled down his temple. "It sounded oh so interesting."

"No-nothing," he stammered. I hummed noncommittally. "I swear, Drusilla. It was nothing."

I pressed the tip of my finger down until the coppery scent of blood met my nose. "I'm afraid I just don't believe you."

"It was the hunters," he burst out. "The same ones you saw me with in the woods the other day." I retracted my nail from his throat at that little tidbit of news and he took the opportunity to spin away from me. He held up his hands, keeping a careful eye on me. "I knew you were there after I saw the boars. Those dumbasses," he shook his head, "They wouldn't know a wolf kill from a bear kill, much less that those two boars didn't kill each other."

"You didn't say anything," I commented, clicking my still lethally sharp nails together as I considered this new information.

"No, I'm not stupid," he retorted, his jowls jiggling as he dabbed the sweat off his forehead. "Your Gran would have strung me up by my ball sack."

I raised an eyebrow. "I can assure you she would have done far worse."

He nodded, staring at me with new respect. "You're right." He swallowed hard. "I underestimated her."

I rolled my eyes. "Everyone does." I pointed a finger at him. "But I'm more interested in why you're still talking to the hunters. You don't have anything they want."

A flash of regret crossed his face and adrenaline surged through me. "She'll kill me, I know that." I tensed, prepared to shift but he was faster, the dart silent as it hit me and I crumpled slowly. He walked up to me, but I couldn't move. "I'm sorry, Dru. I am." He shook his head. "They don't pay if you don't show up with the goods," he explained, patting my hand. I could feel his touch but couldn't react and rage splintered through me. "Margaret says the boy needs medicine. Medicine that cost money. Selling wolf shifters is the only way to make money." I wanted to argue, but speech was impossible, and all I could manage was a grunt and he closed his eyes. "At least you can rest easy knowing your Gran will kill me for what I am about to do."

I wasn't about to *rest easy* knowing he was selling me to hunters completely helpless, not when I was regretting not killing him myself. I tried to move my limbs to no avail, wiggling my fingers was impossible and I wanted to scream in frustrated rage, but I couldn't do that either! He hooked his arms under my shoulders and started to drag me, my butt bumping over every root. I heard him panting in exertion and wanted to yell at him that I didn't weigh that much.

Dru? Paige's sleepy voice broke through my internal ranting and I didn't hesitate.

Go back to sleep.

Where are you?

Patrolling, I lied, wincing internally when a broken branch caught on my leg, slicing the skin open.

You're lying.

No, I'm not.

Yes, you are.

Go back to sleep, I ordered in exasperation.

What are you hiding? She asked instead, her voice more alert.

Nothing. I swear. I just needed to clear my head. I wasn't lying about the clearing my head part and she must have sensed the honesty because she let it go.

I thought you were in trouble. I was dreaming and you were shouting, she sounded puzzled and I had to calm my heartbeat so I didn't tip her off that everything wasn't alright.

It was just a dream, I assured her.

Okay, she replied, accepting my answer and I ignored the guilt that formed. *I love you.*

I love you, too, I said automatically, hoping it wouldn't be the last time I had a chance to tell her. *I'll see you soon.*

I glared at Strickland since it was about the only thing I could do but he astutely avoided my gaze. This went on for a while, my butt bruised and battered from being dragged, when he stopped to wipe the sweat off his face. He came around, his face flushed and looked at me for the first time. I tried to convey every ounce of the emotions I couldn't express through my eyes and he nodded, glancing away.

"I don't blame you." Fury flashed through me, but he wasn't through. "I'm not proud of this, but I have to take care of my own. If your Gran had just taken care of you when you were born…..well none of this would be necessary." My blue eye started to glow and he stepped back warily. "Look, what I gave you will wear off in about two hours. They don't know that." He must have read the question in my eyes because he looked away. "I know what you've done for the village. Your hunting has been the difference between life and death for most. They might not know it, but I do." Some of my anger drained away. "If it wasn't for my grandson, I wouldn't do this." I could see the sincerity in his eyes and had to look away. I understood exactly how far a person would go for someone they loved. "I can die in peace," he continued and a niggle of regret worked its way through me, dissolving the last of my anger, but there was nothing I could do to change his outcome. He'd made his choice and now I had to make my own.

He backed away slowly, leaving me lying there paralyzed, but now I knew I had a fighting chance. I just needed to bide my time.

Chapter Fourteen

Caleb

I planted my feet on the ground, my back cracking as I stretched, unused to sleeping in an actual bed. I patted the soft mattress, unable to stop myself from imagining Dru sprawled across it. I squeezed my eyes shut, pinching the bridge of my nose, but it did nothing to wipe the image from my mind, my memory bringing every detail of her body into focus, including the scent of her. My eyes popped open to make sure she wasn't actually there, but only wrinkled sheets met my gaze and I shoved myself off the bed, my body uncomfortably tight.

A knock on the door had me reaching for a pair of sweats as I called, "One sec." I had no idea who might be on the other side of the door and had no intention of giving Dom's kids an eyeful. Nudity was a natural state for shifters but I hadn't run with the Pack in….I started adding it up in my head and a sigh gusted out of me. Too long. The answer was too long.

I pulled the door open, instantly grateful I'd decided on pants when a pair of golden eyes stared up at me. "Hi," I said as she thrust something in my hand and then darted down the hall. "Bye," I said to no one as I shoved the cookie she'd given me in my mouth and followed her down the hall.

Pure chaos met me as I entered the kitchen. Dom had a kid hanging upside down on his arm, Jess was putting platters of food on the table, and there was half a dozen kids milling around. My forehead crinkled as I asked, "How many kids do you have?"

"They're not all mine," Dom answered, trying to wrestle the kid he held into a high chair. "We're babysitting."

"Oh."

"Sit down," Dom yelled fruitlessly as kids dashed around him. "Come on. It's almost time to eat." I snitched a piece of bacon off the platter and Jess gave me a warning stare but didn't comment.

"Can I help?" I asked, not entirely sure the past ten years had prepared me for domestic hell. Jess shook her head and pointed at a chair which I took to mean, sit down so I did. Dom managed to get the little one strapped down, but kids still raced around the table.

"Everybody find a seat," Dom said again, frustration lacing his voice, but none of them obeyed.

"Sit down," Jess ordered, her voice cracking over the chaos like a whip and there was an instant scraping of chairs as they rushed to obey. "Caleb first," she added, indicating I should fill my plate and Dom just sat back, shaking his head ruefully.

"I might be Alpha, but we all know who's in charge," he commented, a besotted smile on his face as he watched his mate and I couldn't help but laugh.

"At least you know your place." I crunched down on the bacon, my plate overflowing as the others filled their plates, and leaving enough left for seconds. Silence reigned as we devoured our food and I accepted when Jess dumped the last of the eggs on my plate.

"More?" She questioned when I finished it and I shook my head no. "You sure? You look like you missed a few meals."

I chuckled and wiped my mouth. "I'll never look at a can of Spam the same way again," I commented and her expression turned puzzled. "It was…you know what – never mind." I found myself reluctant to talk about my time with the Ghost Pack and Dru. Thoughts of her were painful, but more than that they were mine and I wasn't ready to share.

"Alright, everybody out," Dom stated, standing up and there was a scurry as the kids all took off and Jess slowly stood, smiling as she kissed his jaw.

"You don't fool me one bit, Dominic Navarre." She pinched his cheek hard and picked up the little kid struggling to get out of the high chair. "You just don't want to keep up with the kids."

"Tell Monster to keep an eye on them," he suggested. "They love it when Dylan plays."

She arched an eyebrow. "Not a bad idea. It's like you've done this a time or two." He swatted her butt and she dodged out of the way, her finger wiggling my way. "And you, you better still be here when I come back."

"Yes, ma'am." I picked up my plate and brought it to the sink, turning on the water as Dom attempted to carry every plate on the table at one time. "How many times have you dropped them?"

"Only once," he grumbled as several dishes slid with a clatter into the sink. He quickly checked to see if any had broken, grinning at me when he realized they were all good. "See? Faster."

"Uh huh." I started scrubbing and rinsing as he picked up the table and then started drying. "I'm fine, you know."

He made a noncommittal noise, and muttered, "I didn't ask." I slide my gaze sideways and he rolled his shoulders. "It's not like you died or anything." He turned then, crossing his arms over his chest, reminding me size wise he could crush me, as he added, "Except, you did."

I nodded, my mouth twisting as I turned to face him. "What do you want from me?" My eyes still only came to his chin even after I'd grown four inches, and I tilted my head up to look at him. "I should have told you were I was, what I was doing, but I didn't expect to be taken prisoner."

"Exactly, you didn't know what you're walking into," he growled. "It's why we created the system in the first place. So I'd know you were safe."

"Trent…"

"Is not responsible for you," Dom interrupted. "I am. And I can't do that again. Feeling you die once was enough, twice was," he paused, his jaw working, "Let's just say there better not be a third time. You get me?" I nodded, dropping my gaze at the reprimand in his voice. He exhaled. "Alright, I'm done."

A grin tugged my mouth as I said, "Sure? I feel like you could yell at me longer."

"Don't tempt me," he snapped, stacking the dry plates and pans. "You want to talk about her?" I gripped the sink at his question, my fingers whitening as I shook my head. "I'm here when you're ready." I managed a nod and he clasped my shoulder. "There's a meeting in a few hours. Gregory's going to tell the story of how we came to be. Everyone will be there."

"Count me in," I replied hoarsely and Dom nodded, stepping away. "The mating bond," I burst out and he stopped, waiting for me to continue and I stared down at the white sink. "Have you ever heard of a pair recreating the mating bond after breaking it?"

A low whistle escaped him and I saw him start to shake his head out of the corner of my eyes before he stopped himself. "I've never heard of anyone surviving a broken mate bond to be honest."

"It wasn't sealed," I told him, meaning we hadn't had sex to finish the bond.

"Even then, that's almost a formality. It's the mental link that would concern me," Dom replied and I nodded in understanding. "I don't know for sure, but maybe talk to Sam and Payne," Dom offered and my eyes shot to his. He shrugged. "Like I said, I don't know for sure."

"Thanks."

"Anytime, Caleb." His hand grazed the back of my head and I ducked out of habit. "I'm glad you're here." I didn't look at him, hearing the choked quality of his voice and he cleared his throat before leaving the room.

The silence echoed with everything I'd missed and the need to escape pressed in on me, but this time I knew exactly where I wanted to go. I grabbed a shirt out of the box left by the backdoor and went outside, my feet taking me unerringly to the edge of the forest.

"Want some company?"

Liam appeared by my side and I cast him a sideways glance. "You got watchdog duty?"

He smiled, but didn't answer, dogging my steps as I kept walking. "Thought we might catch up."

"I visited fifteen packs across the country, ending with the Ghost Pack to the north where I met my mate and died, but…spoiler, I came back and here I am," I summarized, lengthening my stride as my need to hurry intensified. Liam kept up, but I noticed his limp grew more pronounced and I stopped, spinning around. "Look, I'm not leaving Pack land. You don't have to follow me. Or pretend like you care."

"This is gonna come as a shock, but it's not pretend," he retorted, positioning himself so his weight wasn't on his bad leg. "We all felt it, Caleb. It wasn't just Dom, and this will probably shock you as much as it did me, but feeling your light fade….we mourned. It was losing a brother, one I don't particularly like but still want to keep around," he finished, his lip curling. "You know what it's like to lose a Pack mate and an Alpha," he reminded me unnecessarily. "So sue me if I want to check on you." He turned, about to go back and I coughed. His head swung toward me, but he didn't turn back, waiting to see if I was actually going to say something.

"I'm going to the burial grounds," I admitted, shoving my hands in the deep pockets of the sweatpants. "I could use the company." He nodded, swinging back around as I hunched my shoulders, unused to having another shifter at my side after years of roaming, but surprisingly, the position wasn't an uncomfortable one. "How's Leah?"

"You suck at small talk," Liam informed me and I nodded in acknowledgement. "But she's good. She's a veterinarian now," he said proudly. He gave me a meaningful smile. "Specializing in Canis Lupus to the never ending confusion of her father."

"Your leg?" He'd broken it years before in a car accident and been forced to shift before it could be set properly, leaving him with a permanent limp.

Liam shook his head, grimacing slightly. "It's a great barometer, but there's nothing we can do to fix it. Trust me, Leah has tried." I wondered if Paige could fix it, but didn't mention the possibility to him since I wasn't sure if they'd ever have a chance to meet and I didn't want to get his hopes up over a long shot.

We strolled silently until we came to the first tree which was also the oldest. I bowed my head, murmuring a blessing, as Liam hung back. Wind whispered through the bare trees and I lifted my head, entering the burial grounds of our Pack. I glanced over my shoulder but Liam just stood respectfully at the edge of the grove. He was originally a Hanley and so none of his family were laid to rest here, not that I thought he'd visit their graves anyway since he had no love for his former family.

The tree had grown since we'd planted my father's bones beneath it, but there was no mistaking the cottonwood. Staring at the thick branches, I waited for something to come to me, for the words I'd never been able to say when he was alive to suddenly spill forth, but there was nothing. I crouched, picking up a handful of dirt and letting it run through my fingers, as I finally said, "I came back."

The words were petty, but honest and I sighed, rubbing the dirt between my fingers.

"You should have trusted me, Dad." I glanced at the older tree next to him, the one that had been planted years before I'd been born, the bench sitting underneath it worn with use. "I didn't understand it, you know, how much you loved Payne's mom. Why you favored Payne over me, but," my chest squeezed tight as I thought about Dru, "I get it now. She was it for you and my Mom was just a poor substitute. Still don't make it right how you treated her though." Old, familiar bitterness coursed through me at the memory of Mom leaving and Dad forcing me to stay, binding me with an Alpha order to make sure I never left Pack land. All because his true mate had died and the son he'd had with her wasn't a shifter, which meant Payne would never become Alpha.

"I don't think it worked out the way you wanted," I told him, pushing to my feet. "Life rarely does, but Payne is happy and I'm getting there so I'm not going to be bitter anymore. You did what you did and it's done now." Weight I hadn't known I carried slipped from my shoulders and I breathed a little easier. I turned, ready to walk away, when I paused to tell him, "I have a mate." A smile creased my cheek as I considered the two of them meeting. "You'd hate her, that's for sure, but she'd like you out of sheer spite. She's complicated like that." I touched the trunk of the tree, the bark rough under my fingertips, and laid our past to rest. "Goodbye, Dad."

Liam stood were I'd left him, his gaze sweeping over the trees, silently counting. He whistled quietly as he finished. "How old is this place?" He asked, his voice hushed. I glanced around, memories of coming here with Dad and Payne flashing through my mind.

"Over five hundred years," I answered, each tree standing as a marker for a deceased Pack member. "Every Pack member is buried here, not just the shifters."

"You honored them all," he whispered in awe.

"Returned to the earth so their wisdom can continue to guide and shelter us under their canopy." I bumped his shoulder. "Now, let's go hear the story of how we came to be."

Liam nodded, but his gaze lingered on the trees, some ancient and others barely a decade old. Something in his expression tipped me off and I grasped his shoulder. "You will be buried here, Leah too."

"I'm not..." he swallowed, the protest dying in his throat as I curled my lip, baring my teeth at him.

"You are." I shoved him forward. "Now, let's go."

***

The round community house was packed when we got there, every man, woman, and child squeezed onto rough wooden benches circled around an open center. Dom and Anna stood in the middle with Gregory and a few of the other Pack elders. Dom motioned to me and I made my way to his side, Liam right beside me.

Everything okay? Dom asked silently as we drew near.

Yeah, just paid Dad a visit, I answered and he nodded, appearing unsurprised. Liam's gaze scanned the room, searching for Leah, and Dom pointed to the corner. I followed his finger and saw Leah bouncing, craning her neck to look around the room. Liam took off the second he saw her, not sparing a backwards glance for us.

I took in the curve of her belly and leaned toward Dom. "Is there something in the water here?" He snorted, shaking his head as Anna stepped forward, her eyes crinkling at the corners as she smiled warmly, her hands outstretched to me.

"Welcome home, Caleb."

"Anna," I greeted her, kissing her cheek and a low growl vibrated the air. I leaned back, releasing her hands as one side of my mouth lifted. "It's been too long."

Trent stepped between us, edging me further away and Anna leaned around him, laughing as she patted his flat stomach. "Excuse my husband, he gets jealous easily."

"I'm not jealous," Trent denied, but he didn't move and Anna's laughing gaze met mine.

"It's really good to see you," she said. "I'm sorry I couldn't join the rescue team."

I chuckled, shaking my head dismissively. "No worries." I gestured to Trent. "He had it covered."

"Your girl….I've met her," Trent disclosed and Anna didn't look surprised so he must have already told her about Dru. "She was the one who warned me away when I visited the first time."

This didn't surprise me considering Dru's panic when Trent had said he'd been there. "I think she's been scaring away shifters for a long time."

"She didn't scare you," Anna declared slyly and I grimaced.

"Not for lack of trying." I glanced at Trent curiously. "Did you ever hear voices in the forest?"

His face grew contemplative and finally he shook his head. "No, I don't recall hearing anything. That was one of the reasons it was so strange. There was this overall feeling of wrongness, the sensation that there was something else out there and it wanted me gone."

I nodded, knowing firsthand what he meant and Anna eyed me like I was crazy. "And you *wanted* to go there?"

I shrugged defensively. "It always intrigued me. There was this Pack that was so close but we knew nothing about them. Or at least no one told us about them," I corrected, frustration lacing my voice. I didn't mention how I'd felt drawn to the Ghost Pack, to the place labeled off limits, and now I knew it was because Dru had been there. She'd called to me, still did, and I was determined to get back to her.

"Welcome," Gregory's deep voice somehow managed to carry over all the buzzing conversations, silencing them instantly.

I really wish I had that ability, Dom murmured over the Pack link and I looked down, hiding my grin.

Maybe when you hit the hundred mark, I joked, keeping my expression neutral and my eyes alert as Gregory's gaze swept over me. It felt like I was finally about to get some answers, the missing piece of a puzzle, one that would allow me to be with Dru.

"Thank you all for coming today to hear my little history lesson," Gregory began with a self-deprecating smile. "I trust it will help put the little ones down for their naps." A few chuckles met his words, relieving the tension that had built in the room. "The history of our people has been passed down from father to son," he paused and smiled at Anna, "And now mother to daughter."

His smile faded as a faint regret filled his expression. "But there is one story, the story of our beginnings, which has been left out." An air of expectancy grew and I waited to see if he'd mention my father's role. "It's time you knew how the wolf and the man became one." The stiffness in my shoulders eased and Gregory settled on a low wooden stool Dom had brought out. "Long ago man and wolf walked side by side, together but separate," Gregory's hands moved with the flow of his words, mesmerizing the room. "The wolf stood as companion to the man, showing himself as a fierce protector and the man returned the favor, providing shelter and food for his four legged friend. They shared their life's journey, working as one. They provided a necessary balance between man and beast, each guiding the other." The wrinkled folds on his face deepened as his voice lowered. "They would die for one another."

"One night they were woken by the rustling of a fearsome beast. It had huge paws *twice* the size of any they'd ever seen," Gregory lifted one hand as the Packs watched with wide eyes. "Razor sharp fangs elongated out of its mouth." He bared his own teeth as some sucked in quick breaths. "And it stood taller than the tallest sycamore tree." One of the children whimpered and his mother quickly quieted him.

"The very sight of this beast froze them in place as they hoped it would leave them in peace." Gregory shook his head slowly. "But it wasn't to be." His arms lowered as we hung on his every word. "The beast attacked," Gregory leapt from his seat and everyone jerked back, one little girl letting out a shrill scream. "He slammed one huge paw into the man, knocking him down, but before he could tear into him, the wolf stepped between them."

Gregory's face grew dark, his eyes glittering as he stalked the room. "The wolf stood ready, fur bristling, his eyes glowing as he protected his fallen friend." We listened, enthralled as he painted a vivid picture of the valiant wolf. "The beast was confused by the wolf, as his snapping jaws kept the beast at bay long enough for the man to stand. They had no weapons to defeat this monster, only a slumbering fire and brave hearts."

"The man grabbed a long stick, stirring the fire's embers until sparks flew into the night air and the beast began to back away in fear. The wolf edged forward, his growls low and threatening as he stood between the man he called friend and the beast. The man threw more logs onto the fire, desperate to scare the beast away before he killed them, and as the wood began to flame, the beast lashed out."

Gregory stopped, making his way slowly back to the stool as every single person in the room waited impatiently, their faces intent. He carefully sat, resting his hands on a cane in front of him. "The wolf yelped in pain as the beast clawed out his belly, and the man charged the beast, a war cry erupting from his throat as he shoved the burning stick he held right into the belly of the beast."

Gasps erupted around the room and one boy cried out, "The wolf. What happened to the wolf?"

Gregory's expression grew long. "It was a killing blow. The man fought off the beast with nothing more than a torch, but it was too late for the wolf. His courage had cost him and he lay on the ground, his belly sliced open as his guts spilled out." Leah's hand rested on Liam's stomach where a long gash hinted at his own near death from the same type of wound. "The man fell to his knees by his wounded companion, tears falling from his eyes as he cried out for help, but it was a deep forest, one that had never been explored by man."

"He feared no one would hear his cries as his friend lay dying, but he wouldn't leave him. They had been through too much together for him to let his friend die alone. So he laid down next to him." A single tear slipped down Gregory's cheek. "The fire burned for three days and nights as the man and wolf laid there, each breath more jagged than the last as the light slowly faded from the wolf's eyes, but still the man didn't move, unwilling to let his wolf take his final breath alone."

More than a few wiped tears from their own eyes, each of us acutely feeling the presence of our wolf. "The fire began to die down as the wolf struggled for breath, his life almost gone, when a cloaked figure entered the small clearing. The man scrambled up, standing protectively over his dying friend as the cloaked figure stopped and drew back the hood covering their face. The man gasped for he'd never seen one such as this, hair white as snow, eyes bluer than the afternoon sky, and his wolf whimpered as the scent of lightning filled the air."

A chill shivered down my spine at his description and Dom moved restlessly as Gregory continued his story.

The man stared at the woman in shock, positive he'd fallen into a dream for what else could explain a woman here, in this lost forest. She came closer and he fell to his knees at the power that pulsed from her.

He pleaded, asking her, "Who are you? What are you doing here?"

She halted in front of him, her eyes glowing unnaturally as she cocked her head. "You called me," she answered and her hand swept out, gesturing to the dying wolf. "May I?"

Desperation filled him and he nodded, allowing her closer. She kneeled, her hands hovering over the wolf for long minutes before she lowered them, shaking her head sorrowfully. "The wound is too severe. I cannot heal him."

The man bowed his head, the pain a burden too great to bear. He buried his hands in the fur of the wolf's neck, meeting the gaze of those intelligent eyes, now cloudy with death. "I'm sorry," he choked out, despair filling him as the last of his hope faded.

"Your pain does not go unnoticed," the woman spoke again, her voice echoing oddly in his ears. "I cannot save his life, but I can preserve it."

The man raised his head slowly, a faint hope stirring in his chest as he met those eerily bright eyes. "What do you mean?"

Her gaze brightened, forcing him to look away. "It will require a sacrifice from you."

He nodded, his stare going back to the wolf. "Anything," he agreed without hesitation.

"It will hurt," she warned and his shook his head dismissively.

"Do it."

She dipped her head, one hand resting on the wolf and the other going to his head. Heat built inside of him, increasing until it reached a white hot crescendo, and knocking him to the ground. Bone and muscle twisted, arching his back as his mouth opened in a silent scream, and he collapsed back, panting as he detected another presence in his mind – a familiar one. He turned his head, but the wolf was gone, and he forced himself up, panicked until a whisper drifted through his mind. His heart raced as he met the gaze of the woman.

"Man and wolf are now one. You share one body, your lives intertwined," she explained, gracefully rising as he remained sprawled on the ground. "He is with you," she commented and he nodded, recognizing the presence inside of him as the wolf.

The man now had the heart and soul of the wolf.

***

It was hard to breath as Gregory finished, knowing the truth now and understanding why my wolf responded to Gran's command. Dom glanced at me, asking, *How powerful are they?* I knew who he meant when he said *they*, but I shook my head, unable to answer without betraying Paige and Dru.

Powerful didn't begin to describe what they were capable of individually much less together and their Gran? She was lethal.

"Magic created us," Gregory spoke and my attention jerked back to him. "And it still resides inside of us. We use it every time we shift and when we heal." His expression turned serious. "Never forget it is a gift."

Hushed whispers broke out in the room and Anna stepped forward. "Thank you for coming today. We've learned a lot and I think it will be good if we take some time to think about it and reconvene later for discussion." It was a clear dismissal and several stood, slowly shuffling from the room. I waited until the room was almost empty before turning to Gregory.

"Are they....?" I paused, reluctant to say what I was thinking, but Gregory knew.

"Witches," he answered as Leah and Liam walked up to us. I took Leah's proffered hand, happy to see her again.

"Congratulations," I told her, nodding to her belly. "And for becoming a veterinarian. We could use you."

She smiled excitedly. "I can't wait for my first patient." We all looked at her and she hastily explained, "I mean a checkup of course. No emergencies." Her eyes widened as she assured us, "But I'm prepared if there *is* an emergency."

"We've all seen you work under pressure, I have no doubt you're ready," Jess told her with a warm smile.

"Good to see you home, son," Hank Navarre declared, dragging me into a bear hug. Bear hug wasn't an exaggeration since Hank was as big as a bear. I thumped his back as he squeezed hard enough to break bone. "I missed you."

"I missed you," I replied truthfully, releasing him reluctantly. Hank had been a second dad to me, the dad I'd wished I'd had, and it wasn't until this moment I realized how much I'd missed him. "Still sheriff?"

He threw back his head and laughed. "That much hasn't changed," he assured me, smiling.

"Dad," Dom said, shaking his head as he grinned wryly. "I see you found your favorite son."

"I claim no favorites," Hank retorted and both of us laughed, and he gave us an offended stare. "What do you mean?"

"I think they mean me, Dad." Sam came up behind him, her yellow eyes a perfect match to Dom and Hank's. She smiled at me. "It's good to see you."

"You too," I answered, distracted by her husband, my half-brother, as he walked toward me. "Payne," I greeted him with a nod and he halted mid-step, standing still for a moment before awkwardly leaning in to give me a hug. I brought my arms up hesitantly, surprised by the warmth of his welcome. He stepped back, swallowing hard, a suspicious red lining his eyes.

"It's….it's good to see you, Caleb." Payne inhaled deeply, glancing down for a second, before meeting my gaze. "I know our relationship hasn't always been the best. Dad…," he paused, grimacing. "You know what? Forget Dad. I want us to be brothers." He very intentionally didn't look toward Dom as he said, "I know I'm not *like* you, but we're still brothers. Family." He blinked hard. "The only family I have left besides Sam and the boys." Sam rubbed his shoulder, her expression fiercely protective and I smiled ruefully.

"I feel like your wife is going to beat me up if I don't accept the olive branch you're offering," I mentioned, eyeing her carefully before glancing back at Payne. "But I'd like that. It's been a long road but they're not wrong when they say all roads lead home." I offered him my hand and when he grasped it, I pulled him into a hug, taking him by surprise. "The past is the past," I whispered and he nodded, gripping my shoulder tightly. We released each other, a new bond tentatively formed, but one I knew had the strength to last.

"We need to talk about the Ghost Pack," Dom stated, his expression apologetic, but I just shook my head, not offended by the interruption. "I only saw one wolf shifter, but there were at least two witches." I bristled at the way he described Dru and Paige, and Jess noticed.

"Dom," she said quietly, resting her hand on his arm. "Let's let Caleb talk," she suggested and he nodded contritely.

"First off, there is no pack," I stated baldly, ignoring them as they exchanged surprised glances. "There's only Dru and she's not....*like* us." I glanced over at Gregory. "Whatever magic protects us when we shift doesn't work for her. She feels everything." His forehead wrinkled, but I didn't wait. "Paige is a witch, a powerful one, but she's tied to the land. I don't completely understand it, but she can't leave."

"The one who spoke telepathically," Monster verified and I nodded. "She's deaf?" He questioned and I nodded again. "There's something about her," he admitted and I wasn't the only one who noticed his interest. Dom closed his eyes and Jess pressed her lips together in an effort to hide a smile.

"Alright, let's get back to it," Dom ordered, gesturing to me.

"Gran, or Mildred is their great grandmother and she is insanely powerful," I warned and Gregory nodded in agreement. "Dru has some ability but there's a lot of tension because she is a shifter." I frowned. "They consider her a mutant." There were a few rumbles of dissent until Gregory stepped forward.

"Wolves and witches don't mix," he declared and a mutinous expression crossed Monster's face. I opened my mouth to protest when Gregory lifted a finger. "Hear me out. I don't mean they can't be together. I mean the gifts we each possess don't mix. I saw your Dru and she is….exceptional and *rare*. The existence of a witch and wolf in the same body is unheard of to be honest."

I nodded reluctantly. "They fear her."

"Probably with good reason." My jaw locked and he raised his hands. "I'm just saying a creature with two powerful abilities would be feared."

"She's not a *creature*," I gritted out between clenched teeth. "She suffers with every shift. She risks her life to feed them and they shun her." I stopped abruptly, hearing the impassioned note in my voice. "She is more wolf than witch. Her ability can't be compared to her sister or grandmother."

"It doesn't mean some won't try," Anna murmured astutely. "Either way, now that we know about them, what do we do?"

"We protect them," I stated quickly, reminding them unnecessarily, "Dru is my mate." I sucked on my lower lip thoughtfully. "I just have to figure out how to convince her that she wants to be," I added under my breath.

"Protecting them might be difficult when they don't want our help." Dom glanced at me. "And I'm not inclined to help someone who killed you."

"Killed?" Several voices echoed at once, those who weren't part of Dom's Pack.

"Rumors of my death have been greatly exaggerated," I muttered, glaring at Dom. "And Paige *saved* my life, so yeah, they deserve our protection."

"Who or what are we protecting them from exactly?" This time it was Trent who spoke and I didn't want to admit the only person they might need protection from was their Gran.

"Dru mentioned there were hunters. They killed her father," I told them, feeling a ripple of unease go through everyone. "I doubt they disappeared." I leaned against the wall. "I've heard rumors."

"What kind of rumors?" Hank asked, his dark eyebrows pulling down.

"Rumors of auctions. It's not enough to just have a wolf shifter. Now they're looking for the *unique*, wolves that are outside the norm," I explained, disgusted. "Someone like Dru."

"Or Dylan," Monster murmured, the deep brown of his eyes turning almost black at the thought. "If there are hunters out there coming after wolves, *special wolves*, then we need to stop them."

"Whoa, hold on a minute," Dom advised, raising his voice slightly. "We don't know that is what's happening here. Let's back it up a second."

"We need to keep an eye on the situation," Jess stated, eyeballing Monster when he grunted. "And not go off halfcocked without knowing all the facts," she stressed when he continued to look rebellious.

"They're right," I added, trying to smooth the situation I'd accidentally created. "They're only rumors."

"You think it's more than that," Monster accused, twisting toward me. "We can't ignore it. What do you think would happen to someone like Paige if they found out about her?"

My jaw worked. "The same thing that would happen to Dru."

"It would be difficult for any hunter to hurt a witch," Gregory said flatly. He eyed me. "You've seen first-hand what they can do. But we do have an obligation to protect them."

All eyes turned to him and he sighed heavily. "Our very existence is in thanks to the first witch. Through the years our lines have multiplied while the witches have died out, partially due to persecution, and also because they were never a fertile line." A flicker of regret crossed his face. "Mildred was once a friend and I failed her. It's time I rectified that."

"You have some scary friends," Trent mumbled under his breath and someone snorted in agreement. A chuckle rippled through the room, breaking some of the tension.

Gregory smiled widely, transforming his face as white teeth flashed. "You have no idea, pup." None of us missed the undercurrent of truth in his words and Trent nodded respectfully. Gregory turned serious as he said, "Anna, I need to request your permission to leave the Pack."

She looked startled at first then shook her head in confusion. "Gregory, you don't need my permission to go anywhere. You're our oldest member. You can come and go as you please." Gregory's expression softened and Anna's mouth formed an O. "That's not what you meant." She blinked rapidly, her eyes growing glossy. "You mean….*leave*, as in no longer a member of my Pack." He dipped his head and Trent came up behind Anna, rubbing her arms as we all stood by silently witnessing the moment. "You've been a member….forever. Is it something I did?"

"Anna, no," Gregory reassured her, taking her hands. "I'm honored to serve under you. It's been a privilege to have you as my Alpha. I don't make this decision lightly."

"Then why?" Anna cleared her throat as she got her emotions under control. "There's no reason for you to go."

A gentle smile wreathed his face. "It's something I need to do, Anna." She shook her head. "I'm going back to the Ghost Pack." I jerked reflexively and Dom tensed. "I need to repair the relationship with Mildred and create an alliance we can all trust. It's necessary for the continued well-being of our Packs." His gaze strayed to me. "Caleb has claimed a mate without a

Pack, one whose unique heritage will require compromise from all of us if she is to join one of our Packs."

"That still doesn't explain why you need to leave *this* Pack," Hank commented, his expression drawn and glancing around I noticed mine wasn't the only concerned face. "You can go as an *authorized*," he gave me a pointed glance, "representative of our joint Packs."

"Witches aren't like wolves," Gregory explained. "They don't travel in packs, they're solitary creatures passing down their power from one generation to the next. Mildred has shown her dislike for wolf shifters. Approaching her as a member of a large, strong Pack will not encourage her to communicate."

"I would agree." Several gazes swung toward me. "Mildred took the Pack from her husband who was Alpha, back when there was a Pack and she kept control of it until Dru was born."

"Then what happened?" Monster asked, his curiosity not going unnoticed by the others.

"She released anyone who couldn't or wouldn't accept Dru on the threat of death. Several left," I said shortly.

"Can we just go back to the part where she *assumed control of a wolf pack*?" Liam questioned, sounding disturbed. "I didn't even know that was possible."

"Trust me, it is," I replied. "She can control the magic of our shift."

Dom rubbed his forehead, shaking his head. "No, just no. No to all of this." He looked straight at me. "She *killed* you. The risk is too great."

"That's not your decision to make," Gregory reminded him and Dom spun around.

"Anna, tell me you're not going to consider this? Not knowing what they're capable of?"

"Dom," she murmured, sounding torn. She glanced at Gregory. "I don't know. Maybe you should stay part of the Pack so we can monitor the situation."

"That won't work," Gregory and I said in unison.

"Can you give us a minute?" Dom motioned for me to follow him and as we left the room I saw Jess catch Monster by the arm. Once we were out of earshot he bombarded me with questions. "Do you really think this is a good idea? Gregory going in alone? After what happened to you?"

"There's more to it."

Dom pinched the bridge of his nose. "Of course there is."

"I did a blood exchange with Mildred."

His expression froze as he lowered his hand, revealing a yellow eyed glare. "You what?"

"It was spur of the moment. I had no idea if it would work," I confessed defensively.

"*Did* it work?"

"Yeah, sort of," I hedged and he lifted his eyebrow. "I was able to resist her command, but it was only once."

"So, you don't know if was a fluke or something to do with the blood exchange," Dom determined and I nodded. "That was a hell of a risk to take."

"I would have killed her if I had known it wouldn't affect Dru. This seemed like a better alternative," I said flatly.

Dom exhaled, nodding. "You're thinking Gregory could do the same thing."

"Maybe," I responded. "It's worth a shot."

"For the record, I still think this is a terrible idea," Dom stated bluntly and I tilted my head in acknowledgement. "But if you think sending Gregory in alone is the best chance we have of creating some type of alliance with the witches, I'll trust your judgement."

I glanced down, caught off guard by his faith in me. "Gregory seems confident that he can convince Mildred."

Dom gripped my shoulder. "I heard Gregory, but it's your opinion I trust."

"Even after I let you down?"

His mouth twisted ruefully. "I let you down first." My forehead wrinkled and he sighed. "I knew you wanted to visit the Ghost Pack and I resisted. I kept putting you off, even while letting you travel the country."

"Why is that?"

He shook his head. "You know? I don't know why. When Trent came back from their lands, it spooked me. Then your dad died, and somehow it all became connected in my mind." He swallowed, glancing away from me. "I kept having this feeling that if I let you go there then I'd lose you." A self-deprecating laugh huffed from him. "Guess I wasn't wrong."

"You haven't lost me," I contended, crossing my arms over my chest. "I'm not going anywhere. We're talking about Gregory."

"*Right now* we're talking about Gregory, but we both know it's only a matter of time before you go back for Dru," he replied knowingly.

"That doesn't mean I'm leaving the Pack," I argued and he dropped his gaze. "*Am I?*" I asked, the world tilting under me as I considered the possibility. "Am I leaving the Pack? Is that what you're trying to tell me? Dru or our Pack?"

"No." He grabbed me by the back of the neck, shaking me lightly. "No. That's not what I'm saying at all." He tilted my head so we were eye to eye. "I've waited a long time to see you happy." He smiled ruefully. "I just didn't expect your mate to be a different species." I thrust my arm out and he dodged, chuckling before he sobered. "It's just this is the first time in years I've seen you so focused. She's what you want and I support you completely. I just don't want you to think you need to do this alone. We're your Pack, we're here for you."

I nodded. "I know that. It's the reason I came back. I know I can't do this alone, not if I want to do it right," I swallowed the sudden lump in my throat as I admitted, "I want to do this right. I messed up the first time with Dru but there's nothing more important to me than keeping her safe and happy. She feels like home."

"Then we do this….together."

"Together," I echoed as the door to the Pack House opened and Anna and Gregory stepped out.

"Is everything alright?" Anna inquired, looking between us and we nodded. "Gregory says it's time."

"You're going now?" I asked in surprise and he nodded, giving me a shrewd glance.

"No time like the present, otherwise you'll beat me there," he replied, his hands resting on his cane. "And I don't think Mildred will appreciate another surprise visit from you."

"You think she'll be more welcoming to you?" I asked doubtfully, remembering the way she'd blasted him off their lands. "She seemed as happy to see you gone as she was me."

"Let's just say, I know her better than she realizes." He smiled grimly. "If she was as unhappy as she said she was at seeing me, then I'd be dead not limping."

"Comforting," Dom muttered, his gaze sweeping over us. "You two are certifiable."

"I'm going too," Monster announced, appearing behind Dom, Jess hot on his heels.

"No," several voices spoke at once, including Dylan who had been lurking around the corner of the building.

"You can't stop me," Monster said defiantly and Dom's nostrils flared.

"Can't I?" Dom questioned dangerously. "I *am* still your Alpha, am I not?" Monster didn't bend, meeting Dom's gaze unflinchingly. "You are underage and under the custody of your father, who I'm positive doesn't want you running directly into a dangerous and volatile situation." Dom tried a different tactic but Monster wasn't swayed.

"I'm going."

"No, you're not," Jess snapped, tugging on Monster's arm, but he didn't budge from his stare down with Dom. "You are not going. Why would you even want to go? They don't exactly like us."

"Some of them do," he replied and I knew exactly who he was talking about. "She needs my protection."

Jess's eyes narrowed and then she screeched, "This is about a girl?" She threw her hands up and we all flinched. "Of course it is. Of course it's a girl. What was I thinking? You're sixteen so of course….girls."

"You were sixteen when you met Dom," he retorted and she pointed her finger at him, almost poking him in the nose.

"Seventeen going on eighteen, thank you very much and we're mates, totally different situation," she corrected him and he looked down. "It is a totally different situation, right? Right?" She asked a little desperately, glancing at Dom. "Please tell me it's different," she begged and I stared at my feet, not wanting to be the one to tell her. "Oh God, I'm not ready." She crouched, staring blindly at our knees. "I thought I had time….boys take longer to mature." She smacked Monster's shin and he jerked. "Why do you have to be so advanced? Can't you just not do this?"

"I don't know. Can I?" He questioned and she shot up.

"Do not turn this around on me," she threatened and he held up his hands. She had to look up at him since he'd topped six feet at some point while I'd been gone and he still wasn't finished growing. His auburn hair glowed in the sunlight and even with the youthful planes of his face we could see the man he would become. "You don't even know her."

"That's not how this works," he reminded her tiredly. "I heard her in my head. You know that's an indication of a mate bond."

"But she's a witch," I pointed out. "Which means Paige can project her voice. I hear her too."

Monster's gaze snapped to mine and there was no mistaking his hostility. "She's mine," he growled possessively, stepping forward as his eyes glittered with challenge. Dylan was next to him in an instant and I tensed automatically. "You can't have her."

"I don't want her," I replied, holding his gaze. "I want Dru." I narrowed my eyes. "Paige isn't a toy to be fought over," I warned him. "She's an amazing woman and if you want to claim her, then you better make sure you deserve her."

He deflated, all the bluster leaving him in a rush as he dropped his gaze. "She's….important. I can feel it, but I don't understand it." He lifted his shoulder. "I feel this need to protect her."

Dom exhaled loudly as Jess frowned. "Dad's going to be pissed," she muttered, shaking her head. "Of course he and Wren had to take the kids to

Disneyland this week." She wagged her finger at Monster. "You still can't go though."

"She's right," I interjected before he started arguing. "We need to let Gregory go and talk to Mildred." I recognized the stubborn set of his jaw since it matched my own. "I understand how you feel." He didn't look convinced so I opened my connection to the Pack and let my emotions flood through it, not holding back the agony of having to break the mate bond or the clawing need to be with Dru.

He hit the ground as Dom doubled over and still I didn't stop it, letting those emotions flow out, but I was careful not to flood the entire Pack. Jess gripped Dom's arm, her expression panicked. "What's going on?" she screamed, telling me Dom must have blocked her so she wouldn't feel it. My gaze locked with Monster as Dylan whimpered next to him. It was almost cruel, but when he mouthed, "Stop," I did.

Dom slowly straightened and Dylan helped Monster to his feet. "You okay?" Monster asked Dylan, patting his shoulder and he nodded.

"I didn't let him feel it," I told Monster. "He's upset because you were." I shot a glance at Dom. "Sorry. I couldn't stop you from getting blasted."

Dom nodded, hooking his arm around Jess when she started for me. "Don't. He's been through enough," Dom ordered and Jess froze, staring up at him in surprise. "I'm sorry, Caleb. I didn't know. I couldn't even begin to imagine." Lines bracketed his mouth as he swallowed. "Come on. I feel the need to hold you," he told Jess, squeezing her hard enough to make her eyes widen. "Monster, you understand now?" Monster nodded, wiping his mouth with the back of his hand. "Good." He glanced at Gregory. "Be careful."

Gregory nodded silently as Dom escorted Jess away, his arm still wrapped around her tightly. "We'll fix this," Gregory promised me and I nodded, not entirely sure how, but unable to contemplate failure. "Anna, do you release me?"

She nodded, her eyes red, but she didn't allow her emotions to escape as she rested her hand on his shoulder. "Gregory, you are released from this Pack. Free to roam and join another Pack. You will be missed." I could see when she broke the connection because Gregory winced, and I knew the echoing emptiness he must be feeling.

"Thank you," I murmured, appreciating the sacrifice he was making.

"Thank *you*," he replied, surprising me. His mouth curved. "You've given me the chance to fix something I'd long given up on." He inhaled, his smile widening as he looked north. "Even this old dog can learn something new."

"Good luck," I offered, holding out my hand and he took it.

"I'll see you soon," he answered, blowing out a breath as he chuckled. "Feels funny not having the Pack link."

"You're not alone," I stated and he nodded to us before heading to the edge of the forest, casting his cane aside as he shifted into his wolf and disappeared into the tree line.

"I need to go talk to," Anna waved her hand, "People." She leaned against Trent whose expression was hard to decipher. "I can't believe he's gone," she whispered, rubbing her forehead and Trent looked straight at me and this time there was no mistaking the blame in his gaze.

"I didn't make this choice for him," I defended myself but he only shook his head, leading Anna away. "He's never going to like me," I told Monster, who shrugged awkwardly. "You're not going to follow Gregory, are you?"

"No, I'm going home," he answered and I turned to leave, trusting he would do what he said. "Caleb," he called and I paused. "I'm sorry about Dru. I hope it works out." I nodded, shoving my hands in my pockets as I wandered to the cabin at the end of the row of cabins. It used to belong to Dom and then his sister, Sam, but now it stood empty. I didn't really want to deal with anyone so I figured I'd crash there for the night.

I walked up the steps, hearing them creak under my weight, and I hesitated at the door, memories flashing through my mind. I'd spent many nights on Dom's couch, unable to deal with Dad and then later because I couldn't deal with the silence of his absence.

I twisted the knob, pushing the door open, then stopped, as we stared at each other in surprise. "Mom?"

Chapter Fifteen

Dru

It wasn't long before Dumb and Dumber showed up, stomping through the woods with less finesse than a herd of elephants. "You think this is a good idea?" I recognized the young, reedy voice and if I could have I would have rolled my eyes.

"Do I think this is a good idea?" The other idiot repeated mockingly. "I don't know, you think having money is a good idea?"

"These things can kill you," the other one squeaked and my impression of him went up a notch. "And selling them at the auction is dangerous."

"It's paralyzed," the older man dismissed as if that somehow made me less dangerous and I decided to kill him first. "It's not the first time I've done this, ya know."

"It still feels wrong," the kid replied, their voices close but I couldn't see them since I was lying sideways where Strickland had dropped me. "We should just leave these things alone."

"It's easy money and you like money," the other one cajoled and I got the impression he needed the kid for something. Bait, maybe or a patsy, either way, I had no intention of showing mercy. "Besides, it's no different than killing a wolf. We're doing a service."

"They're people though. Aren't' they?"

"If you can call something that turns into an animal people," the other one scoffed. "They don't have brains. It'll kill you in a second. It's worse than an animal."

Rage burned inside of me, eating away at whatever Strickland had injected me with, and I knew it wouldn't be long before I could move.

"Aha, here it is," the other guy shouted gleefully and I heard him stop next to me. "Pretty little thing."

"It's a girl," the kid announced, gulping as he came around to my head. "I didn't know we were getting no girl."

"She'll get a real good price," the other man chortled and his hand touched my hair. I couldn't do anything except glare and the kid stumbled back.

"I don't think she likes you touching her," he said, staring at my blue eye in horror.

"She's paralyzed. What's she going to do?" He questioned, his hand drifting lower and I suddenly wished I had Paige's ability to project thoughts and emotions because I would terrify this bastard.

"Are you sure she's a wolf?" The kid whispered, not taking his eyes off me.

"Yeah, they have girl ones, but they're rare. She's worth a fortune." I heard the greed in his voice as he grabbed one of my arms. "Come on, now. Help me get her to the truck." The kid came up hesitantly, his hand hovering by my arm. "Grab it," the other man ordered and he jumped, taking my arm. Together, they dragged me further through the woods until we came to a dirt track and a pickup truck. "Toss her in the back," the older man grunted. "But don't bruise it. She's worth more not bruised."

"This is a bad idea." I agreed with the kid as one of my toes curled, and a tingling sensation started to trickle through my extremities. This had become a very bad idea…for them. "We should leave her here."

"Hell, no, boy, and if I hear another word out of you, I'll leave you here." The tailgate slammed shut. "Now get in the damn truck before I leave you out here for her friends to find."

The boy scurried to the truck door and I heard two doors slam shut as I tried to wiggle more fingers and toes, but nothing else happened and I resigned myself to wait it out. We drove for a long time on the dirt track, my body bouncing all over the truck bed, until we finally turned onto a gravel road which wasn't much better.

I knew we were headed south, and my heart rate kicked up as the truck slowed, but we just turned onto another road, this one paved. Adrenaline surged through me as I managed to curl my hand into a fist. Just a little longer, I promised myself.

Seconds turned to minutes and I could feel my chest rise and fall, then I could bend my arms and legs. Power surged through me, energizing my muscles and I prepared to launch myself out of the truck. If I could reach the trees then I would be on familiar territory and there was no way they'd get the upper hand. Dense forest lined the road on either side, but we were going fast, too fast for me to jump without hurting myself. I needed to slow them down.

My fingers tingled as power pulsed through me, stronger than I'd ever felt, and I smiled as I spread my hand and the truck started to levitate. I released it and felt the jolt when the tires touched back down. The two idiots in the truck were yelling in panic, and the truck started to slow. My legs tensed, ready to spring out of the truck bed, when the truck swerved, brakes squealing and I was thrown against the cab, my head slamming against metal. Spots filled my eyes, but I couldn't let the opportunity escape me.

A gunshot rang out as I scrambled over the side of the truck and I heard a howl cut off abruptly. I crouched behind the truck as the doors flew open, "What are you doing, Chuck?" The kid shouted, standing behind the door like he was scared of whatever they'd just shot.

"You see the size of this thing?" Chuck shouted, excitement filling his voice and I lowered myself until I could see under the truck and my eyes rounded at the sight of the massive wolf lying on the ground. It was hands down the biggest wolf I'd ever seen and my heart started to hammer as I glanced at the forest. I knew I could make it, but as Chuck started to drag the wolf toward the truck, I knew I couldn't leave it.

"Luke, get over here and help me," Chuck yelled, sounding entirely too happy. Luke edged away from the door, reluctantly going over to Chuck. "We're gonna be rich. Two of 'em. That's gotta be a record."

"Shit," I muttered, slithering back over the truck side as they bent over the humongous wolf shifter. I wasn't sure why it hadn't shifted back into human form, but I also knew I couldn't leave a defenseless wolf at their mercy. I laid back down, trying to remember how I'd been positioned, but it didn't matter as they lowered the tailgate.

"Geez, this thing is a monster," Chuck grunted. "Even dead, it'll fetch a good price. Some dumb fool will want to stuff it." They managed to shove the wolf all the way in and when it's fur brushed against my skin I knew it wasn't dead.

A howl pierced the night and a prickle went through me. Something was out there and it was not happy. The tailgate slammed shut and the men ran to get back into the truck. I stretched my hand out, touching the wolf, and sensed the life fading from him. I shook him gently, hissing, "Shift." I knew a shift would save his life but when he didn't respond I crawled over him. I couldn't go around – he took up the entire truck bed.

Dark fur hid the wound and I ran my hand over his side until I touched wet fur and pulled my hand back to find blood coating my fingers. "Shit," I muttered again, wishing Paige was here. "Why don't you shift?" I grumbled under my breath. "It would save us both a lot of trouble." He didn't hear me or wouldn't respond and I dug my fingers back into his fur until I found the hole in his side.

I breathed shallowly, the scent of blood making my stomach roll, and focused the power dancing through me. I'd never felt it this strong before and wondered if this was what it was like for Paige and Gran all the time. I tried to send the magic rolling through me into the wolf to no avail. "Oh come on, Paige does this all time," I whispered as blood continued to ooze from him, slowing as he lost too much blood. Panic had my heart racing as I glanced at his head, but his eyes were closed. I closed my own eyes, breathing slowly as the magic inside of me coiled, pulsing so strong I was afraid it would kill me if I didn't release it somehow.

Heat swelled under my palm as I held it to the wound and I tried to contain my excitement as I felt it working. "Come on, big boy," I mumbled encouragingly as magic flowed into him, stitching together the gunshot wound until a bullet pressed against my hand as the wound closed completely. I curled my fingers around the bullet, glancing at his head hopefully, but his eyes remained shut even as his breathing steadied. "Okay," I whispered to myself, nodding as the truck accelerated, the lights of a town glowing in the distance and I knew my window to escape was quickly disappearing.

I debated jumping out, but it meant leaving the wolf. I glanced longingly at the forest, desperate to melt into its shadows, I'd done all I could for the wolf, healing it's wound. I couldn't exactly force him to wake up. I grabbed the scruff at his neck, shaking him hard, and his eyes cracked open. "Yes! That's it. Wake up," I encouraged, leaning forward and getting my first true whiff of him that wasn't disguised by blood. I sat back, recognizing the scent as one of the wolves who'd come for Caleb. "You're from his Pack," I murmured, shaking him again as his eyes drifted closed. There was something odd about them.

He didn't open them again though and as we came to a break in the tree line, a flickering sign proclaimed we were passing the Wander Inn Motel. I wasn't familiar with the area, but I figured we had to be either on Pack land or close. The truck didn't slow though, instead speeding up, and I knew I'd survive a jump, but it'd cost me. The unconscious wolf was another problem. He was huge and difficult to move. It was possible I could levitate him out, but I didn't want to risk him getting shot again. There was no way the imbeciles in the truck would miss me levitating an enormous wolf out the back of their truck.

"Shit." I sank back down next to the wolf, patting his shoulder as he remained oblivious to the trouble we were in.

Chapter Sixteen

Caleb

I hugged her, unable to process the fact that she was really there. "Mom," I murmured again, feeling her wrap her arms around my waist. "What are you doing here?"

I felt her chest vibrate with laughter. "I came to see you, son."

"You did?"

"Yes."

"Why?"

"Because you're my son?" She pulled back, smiling up at me. "I missed a lot, Caleb. I'd like to make up for lost time."

"Yeah, okay. I just...no one told me you were here."

"That was intentional," she answered, guiding me to the massive sectional left from when Dom had lived there. "I heard from them that you almost died." I didn't correct her, figuring she didn't need to know that I had actually died. "I wanted you to have time to recover before I sprang myself on you."

"Probably a good idea," I replied, still stunned at seeing her. She'd returned to her Pack years and years ago when I'd still been a child. It wasn't until I was an adult that I'd worked up the nerve to visit her, positive she wouldn't want to see me. I'd been wrong and we'd reconnected, but I couldn't stay with her Pack since I didn't intend to join them. It made visits awkward so it'd been a few years since I'd seen her. "How long are you here for?"

She smiled timidly, revealing faint wrinkles around her eyes that I had never noticed. "Well, that's what I wanted to ask you."

"Me?"

She reached for my hand, squeezing it, as she said, "I want to come back, Caleb. For good."

"Wha....what do you mean?" I stuttered in disbelief. "Join my Pack?"

"Exactly. Either Dom or Anna's Pack."

"You'd leave your Pack to come back here? With all the bad memories?" I questioned, stunned.

"They weren't all bad, Caleb. You've chosen your Pack and truthfully there's nothing holding me to my own Pack. I want to spend time with my son and the only way that can happen is if I come back."

"You would do that? For me?" It seemed impossible that she'd give everything up just to spend time with me, but as she smiled, I could see she would do exactly that.

"You're the most important person in my life, son. Of course I'd do that." She brushed a lock of hair from my forehead, the gesture a familiar one from my childhood, and I had to blink hard. "I missed so much. I don't want to miss anymore. I want to see you become a dad, be a grandmother to your children, and see the amazing man you've become without me."

"With you," I replied. "You've always been with me." I touched my chest as the memories I'd buried deep fought to resurface – the nightly bedtime stories, the gentleness of her touch, and her broken expression when she'd been forced to leave me. "I would love it if you stayed," I said belatedly. "There's someone I want you to meet," I added eagerly.

She smiled, tilting her head as she met my gaze. "Is it a special someone?"

I nodded. "Very special," I agreed, my expression softening. "She's everything I ever wanted."

Mom stroked my cheek. "I'm glad to hear that." Her eyes grew damp. "All I wanted was for you to be happy."

"I am," I assured her. "I'll be happier when I can bring her home, but just knowing she's out there gives me peace."

The door burst open, slamming against the wall so hard it splintered. Monster stood there, completely naked as he panted. "I need your help." He sucked in a deep breath as I leaped to my feet, his voice coming to me over the Pack link. *Two men shot Dylan. They took him in their truck. I followed, but I couldn't stop them. I came to get help.*

Good, you did the right thing, I replied. *Can you pick up their scent?*

He nodded, a red flush highlighting the freckles across the bridge of his nose. I glanced back at Mom and she waved her hands, urging me to go. "I'll alert the others. Go."

I can't reach Dylan, Monster admitted and I gripped his shoulder.

He's okay, I told him, searching the connection until I felt the faint pulse of his life. *He's alive.*

Monster nodded, swiping at his eyes as we left the cabin, and headed to a familiar jacked up Jeep. I hopped into the driver's seat, nodding at him. *You tell me where to go.*

I popped it into gear, peeling down the dirt road that connected our little community to the outside world. I gunned the engine as the road straightened out, and when we hit a bump in the road, the tires left the ground. We bounced as we came back down, fishtailing a little as I took a turn faster than I should, and had to steer us straight as Monster sat tensely next to me. "South," he muttered as I came to the road, but before I could make the turn, someone stepped in our path.

"Shit," I shouted, slamming on the brakes, the back tires spinning as we skidded to a halt sideways. My heart thumped as Trent walked toward us. "What the hell?" I yelled as he swung himself in the back since the top wasn't on. "I could have hit you."

"Good thing the brakes work," he answered mildly and I glanced at Monster, who only shrugged. "We going?"

I hit the gas again, muttering under my breath as we hit the road, leaving black marks as I made the turn too fast. "How'd you know?"

"I don't trust you." He glanced at Monster. "Either of you." He held onto the roll bar as I flew through the only stoplight in town. "I was waiting for you to do something stupid."

"Somebody has Dylan," Monster growled and Trent bent down toward him.

"And how did they get him? Weren't you supposed to be at home sleeping?"

I shot a sideways glance at Monster in time to see the guilt flash across his face. "What were you doing?" I snapped, my tempter starting to flare. "Theo, answer me."

"We were going to the Ghost Pack. I wanted to talk to Paige," he admitted, not looking at us. "But Dylan…he went racing the other way, to the road. I couldn't make sense of his thoughts, but he ran right into the road."

"He knows better," Trent said needlessly. "Dylan is careful. He wouldn't leave your side."

"I know that," Monster burst out. "But something about that truck set him off. I couldn't keep up with him and then I heard a shot." Monster's expression turned to one of self-disgust. "By the time I got there, they had him in the truck. All I could do was follow them." He rubbed his face.

"How many?" Trent questioned as I pressed the accelerator a little harder, shifting gears as we left the town of Banks in the rearview mirror.

"Two," Monster paused. "I think. There might have been someone in the back of the truck." He swallowed, shaking his head. "We have to hurry. Dylan…."

"Yeah, we know." There was no telling what Dylan might do. He was unpredictable and if he had been shot, he might not be able to shift to heal himself. "Can you reach him?" I asked Monster, who shook his head, his expression tight. "Keep trying," I ordered.

The Jeep rocketed down the dark road as I steered us south. There were no other roads so eventually we had to catch up to them, but I started to get nervous as we kept going with no sign of them. "They went this way," I double checked and Monster nodded.

Another few miles and then Trent shouted, "Up ahead." He pointed and I squinted, slowing the Jeep as a truck came into view, the front of it crumpled against a tree, no one in sight. "Is that the truck?"

"Yeah," Monster answered, already leaning out the door of the Jeep in preparation when I stopped. I snagged his arm and he shot me an angry glare.

"We don't know what we're walking into," I reminded him. "Don't go running off."

He nodded and I brought the Jeep to a stop behind the wrecked truck.

"You smell that?" Trent asked and we nodded, catching the scent of blood. "Dylan was definitely here."

Wind swirled the leaves on the ground around us, bringing another scent and I jerked forward as I recognized it. Trent reached for me, but I stumbled out of his reach, walking toward the truck like a zombie, my throat working as my mouth formed a single word, "Dru."

Chapter Seventeen

Dru

The wolf twitched as the truck sped through a tiny town and a spurt of hope shot through me, but he didn't open his eyes. I didn't know where we were going, but our chances of escape decreased with every mile. If they managed to get us to this auction they kept talking about, it would be impossible to escape. Right now, idiots held us but I had a feeling that would change once we got to our destination.

I reached for the wolf's feet, tickling them and he jerked reflexively but didn't wake and I sighed. I was running out of ideas and time, since I didn't know how long it would take to get wherever we were going, and I couldn't wait any longer for the wolf to regain consciousness.

An impenetrable wall of trees lined both sides of the road and there were no other vehicles in sight. I braced myself against the side of the truck, one hand on the wolf as I worked up my nerve. I had one shot at this and there was no margin for error. A deep breath and the truck's tires continued to spin, but there was nothing for them to grab as we went airborne. Chuck panicked, just like I knew he would, jerking the wheel and I released the truck in time for us to slam into a tree.

The impact sent me flying, my hand still locked around the wolf's leg so he went with me, both of us landing somewhere in front of the truck. I gasped, trying and failing to suck air into my lungs. Round eyes met mine and I realized the wolf was awake. I opened my mouth, starting to feel desperate as my lungs refused to work, and his snout nudged my cheek. My eyes drifted closed as he tried to comfort me and as I relaxed, a little bit of air entered my lungs. Each breath came a little easier until I could take a full breath.

I assessed my body, searching for broken bones or hidden damage, but there was nothing. I eased into an upright position to find the wolf sitting on his haunches staring at me unblinkingly. "You okay?" I asked, not expecting a response and I didn't get one. "Thank you," I added gratefully, my gaze straying to the pickup truck currently smooshed into a tree. "I need to see what happened to them." I gestured to the truck but still didn't get any type of response. "Can you shift?"

He blinked and a second later, a man sat there, his distinctive round eyes explaining why he'd been so uncommunicative. "You made that look easy," I grumbled, scrambling to my feet as I tried to avoid looking at anything below his neck. "Blink and you're a man. Another blink and you're a wolf." I limped my way over to the truck, my body protesting the movement, as he trailed behind me silently, and the intensity of his stare made my shoulders twitch.

The kid, Luke, was unconscious, blood trickling down his temple, but old Chuck was wide awake and started screaming when he saw me. "Don't kill me.

Please. Turn me into one of you," he begged and I shook my head. "Please, my leg."

"Chuck, we're not vampires. It doesn't work that way." His eyes widened when he spotted the wolf shifter he'd shot standing behind me and he whimpered. "Besides, even if it did work that way I'd never turn you. I don't like you." I rested my arms on the window of the truck, surveying the damage. "But I will do something for you." Hope flared to life behind his eyes and I smiled. "I'll put you out of your misery." Chuck's head snapped back as the wolf shifter moved faster than I'd ever seen, breaking his neck with no compunction. "I was going to do that," I protested and he lowered his head apologetically and I waved my hand. "It's alright. Dead is dead." The shifter moved, reaching for Luke and I shook my head. "Not him."

The rumble of an engine reached my ears and I moved instantly, dragging Luke out of the truck and awkwardly shuffling to the tree line. "A little help?" I whistled, snapping my fingers at the other shifter as he stood there, staring down the black road. "Hey, I don't want to get caught out here by some Good Samaritan." He lumbered after me, lifting the unconscious man with ease and this time I followed him as we went into the trees, but he wouldn't budge after a few feet. His gaze kept straying back to the road and in an effort to distract him, I asked, "What's your name? I'm Dru."

He stared at me for a second, then said, "Dy-lan."

"Dylan, nice. It's really nice to meet you, Dylan." I leaned over Luke, searching for any injuries, but besides the goose egg on his forehead, he mainly had bruises since the truck had hit on the driver's side. "I'm going to try to heal him," I explained, not wanting to try and make my way through the woods with an unconscious guy and unknown shifter. He just watched me, those innocent eyes curious, as warmth built underneath my hand and Luke's bleeding stopped. A few seconds later, his eyes opened and I saw the instant he recognized me because pure terror glazed his eyes. "I'm not going to hurt you –"

He scrambled backwards, straight into Dylan, and his mouth opened but before he could scream I held out my hand and said, "Silence." His mouth sealed shut and if it was possible he looked even more terrified, and I stared at my hand in surprise. I hadn't really thought that would work. Magic wasn't my gift, I was a wolf shifter, but somehow, something had changed. I slowly opened and closed my hand as Dylan watched me, his gaze surprisingly observant.

The engine rumbled closer, close enough now I could see headlights, and hear as it started to slow down, no doubt seeing the wrecked vehicle. "Stay quiet, okay?" I asked and Dylan sat down next to Luke with a thump, his lips pressed together. "I'm not going to do to you what I did to him," I tried to reassure him, but it didn't seem to help and I sighed. "Okay, good job terrifying people, Dru."

The 4x4 vehicle rolled to a stop and three men got out, the headlights turning them into shadows and the wind blew away from me so I couldn't detect their scent. Friend or foe, I had no idea until I heard a single word whispered on the wind, "Dru."

I was on my feet without realizing it. "Caleb." I started to run, sliding down the embankment and he was there, catching me. "Caleb," I whispered again, burying my face into his neck. "You're here." Strong arms wrapped around me, cradling me gently.

"Are you okay?"

I nodded, the words stuck in my throat.

"Dylan! Dylan," I heard someone cry out and I lifted my head. "Dylan, are you here?"

I pointed to the trees and the other guy launched himself up the hill. "He's okay?" Caleb asked and I nodded again. "I had no idea you were in that truck," he admitted, his voice thick with emotion. "We were trying to save Dylan."

"Luck," I croaked and his arms tightened around me.

"Fate," he corrected and I couldn't exactly argue.

Dylan, Monster and Luke made their way back down to the road as the other guy with them walked up to me and Caleb. He dipped his head to me and I managed a wan smile. The night was catching up to me, the power I'd used saving Dylan and crashing the truck, revealing it's toll and I swayed, only upright because Caleb held me. "Okay, we need to get you home," he decided, scooping me up.

"What do we do with him?" Trent pointed to Luke, who stared at us, his lips sealed shut. "He won't say anything."

"Bring him," I murmured and Caleb shrugged.

"You heard her," he stated and Trent dragged Luke toward the Jeep. Once there, it was quickly apparent there were not enough seats to go around. Monster and Dylan came to the side of the Jeep, as Trent stuffed Luke in the back and Caleb climbed in, settling me on his lap.

"We'll run," Monster stated, solving the seating problem but Caleb glared at him to my surprise.

"Straight home," he ordered them and Monster nodded, not speaking. "I mean it, Theo." He nodded again and Caleb leaned back, waving his hand for them to go. Exhaustion overtook me and my head started to drift forward and I jerked, forcing myself to stay awake. "Easy, Dru. I've got you." Caleb's bright blue eyes met mine. "Sleep. I won't let anything happen to you." I nodded, trusting him to take care of me, as my body shut down, no longer able to function now that the adrenaline had worn off.

Trent hopped into the driver's seat as Luke sat in the back, staring in horrified fascination as Monster and Dylan shifted into wolves and took off to the woods. I rested my head against Caleb as Trent made a wide circle, taking us back the way we came, and finally closed my eyes as the tires rumbled on the road.

***

I woke up to bright sunshine and a warm body curled around mine. I didn't need to see him to know Caleb had stayed with me, his presence a comforting blanket. I stretched my toes, awed by the softness of the sheets. I raised my hand to my face, frowning when I saw blood and dirt crusted on it, and scrambled out of the clean, soft bed.

"Wha- Dru?" Caleb sat up, instantly alert as he glanced around in concern, searching for me.

"I'm dirty," I told him, brushing at the sheets as I tried to get any dirt that may have flaked off of me when I slept. "I don't want to mess the sheets up." He stared at me in disbelief, and captured my hand when I got close.

"It's okay," he assured me, his gaze bleary as he realized there was no danger. "We'll wash them."

"Exactly," I protested. "Washing sheets is my least favorite chore. I usually make Paige do it." Her name brought a sudden stab of alarm. "Paige!"

Caleb shot out of the bed, alarmed. "Was she taken too? We didn't see her."

"Huh?" I cocked my head and he stared back at me, confusion written on his face. "No," I said, catching on. "They didn't take her, but she's probably worried sick about me."

Caleb sank back down on the bed and I noticed for the first time that he wore a random set of clothes, as if he'd just grabbed them from a box or something. "She can wait," he replied. "Gregory has gone to your family lands to try and make peace with your Gran."

"Gregory?" I questioned, not sure which one that was.

"The old one," Caleb answered, adding, "The one who knew Mildred. He called her Millie."

"Oh, okay. Brave of him," I muttered, scratching my arm, the dried blood itchy.

Caleb caught my arm, rotating it carefully, but there was nothing there. "I checked you for injuries, but I couldn't find any. There was so much blood though."

"Not mine," I assured him, as it flaked between my fingers. "The other wolf, Dylan, it's mostly his."

"He was shot?" Caleb questioned and I nodded.

"He was, but he wouldn't shift. I managed to heal him."

"You healed him?"

My gaze flicked down as I said, "I did. It was weird. I've never been able to do that. I felt the power like I've never experienced. It surged through me, like it wanted me to use it." I plucked at the filthy shirt I still wore. "Do you have a bucket and some more clothes?"

"I have clothes," he mentioned, his forehead wrinkling as he asked, "What's the bucket for?"

"So I can clean up."

"You can take a shower," he suggested, pointing to a door I hadn't noticed. "Plenty of hot water. Dom is famous for taking 30 minute showers so they have a tank less hot water heater."

Most of what he said didn't make a lot of sense, but I followed him as he walked over to the door. There was a sink, a toilet, and the biggest shower I'd ever seen. It was like the one we had outside but clean and nice, the walls made of a slick tile and the shower head went into the wall. "Where's the cistern?"

"We don't have one," he replied, twisting a handle on the wall and water came pouring out, steam quickly filling the room. "Just turn it to make the water hot or cold or turn it off."

I stretched my arm out and flinched as the droplets pricked my skin harder than I expected. "It won't run out?"

He shook his head and I smiled excitedly, stripping the shirt over my head. He backed out of the room, keeping his eyes averted, as he said, "I'll go get some clean clothes. Have fun."

I didn't even hear him as I stepped under the stream of hot water as it came down harder than the most torrential downpour. I played with the knob thing, turning it the wrong way and the water turned cold, and I hurried to turn it the other way until the water came out scalding. I scrubbed my skin, then saw a bar of soap, but it wasn't like anything I'd used before, it smelled wonderful and as I rubbed it over my body, bubbles formed on my skin. I used it to wash my hair since it smelled so good, then just stood under the water, letting it rain down over me, and wished I could show this to Paige.

"Dru?" Caleb called through the door, tapping and then opening the door as I continued to stand under the waterfall. "Hey, you coming out? You're going to turn into a prune."

I blinked at him through the water, but steam coated the glass door hiding him from my view. He finally opened the shower door, reaching over to turn the water off. He grabbed a towel, wrapping it around me as he tugged me from the shower.

"That thing is amazing," I told him and his lips curled up. "You should have put me in there before you let me get in the bed and dirty the sheets."

"I'll wash the sheets," he promised, knotting the towel so it wouldn't fall, and I nodded, not arguing since I really hated laundry. His hands framed my face, brushing the wet strands of hair from my cheeks, and intensity radiated from him. "I told myself to wait. To give you time." He shook his head. "I can't. Dru, you are everything to me. Everything I didn't know I wanted. Everything I didn't know I was missing. Giving you up was the hardest thing I've ever done and I know I can't do it twice."

His blue eyes measured my expression and I knew he saw the fear I couldn't contain. "I can't do that again," I whispered, the empty agony of the mating bond still there, a constant reminder of loss. "I wouldn't survive."

"You won't have to," he swore, his eyes almost glowing at the sincerity in them. "I will never do that again. My life is only complete with you. I don't want to live with this emptiness. To wonder what we could have been."

The ache in my chest grew, equal parts fear and hope. "There's so many things we don't know. Gran and Paige. Me. I'm a freak. You don't want to have kids with a mutant." I wanted so badly to give in, to have what he promised with his eyes, but there was no escaping the memory of him severing the bond. Our relationship would never be easy and there was no guarantee he wouldn't do it again, thinking he was protecting me.

"I'd love to have kids with you," he stated, his thumb stroking my temple. "I want to face all of those things with you, by your side, a bonded unit, unbreakable. I want people to see us and dream of one day having what we have."

"I can't lose you. Not again."

"You won't," he vowed. "Everything that comes we will face together as mates."

"You have to swear that for the rest of our lives," I paused and his expression turned serious as he waited for my condition, "That you'll do the laundry."

A smile broke out on his face, revealing the wide smile lines bracketing his face. "That seems only fair, but I have to tell you, we have washing machines." My forehead wrinkled at that revelation, but he didn't bother to explain, his head lowering. He hesitated right before his lips met mine. "Do you accept me as your mate, Dru?"

"Yes," I whispered, brushing my lips against his, and ensuring our fates would always be entwined. His mouth moved over mine gently, exploring every inch as I threaded my fingers through his hair. He trailed his lips over my jaw, lingering at the hollow beneath my ear before using his teeth to tug on my earlobe.

"There's only one way to seal a mate bond," he reminded me, tucking my hair behind my ear as he pressed kisses down my neck, one finger tracing along my collarbone. "When you're ready." He lifted his head, his eyes glittering as a faint flush covered his face.

My hand found the knot holding the towel up and I loosened it as I said, "I'm ready."

He sucked in a breath, his eyes tracing the towel's path as it slowly slid to the floor, and I stood there as the emotions locked behind his eyes started to flood through me. Awe and gratitude, quickly supplanted by pure desire. "You're beautiful," he whispered, his Adam's apple bobbing. His hands hovered above my arms, almost but not quite touching and goosebumps raised on my skin as an electric current seemed to form between us.

His fingers lightly stroked down my arm, sending shivery sparks through me. He brought his hands to my sides, barely touching, but the rough calluses on his fingers made me tremble in anticipation.

"You're sure?" He confirmed and I arched an eyebrow.

"Are you?" More emotion flowed through me from him, an absolute certainty that couldn't be mistaken.

"Nothing I want more," he promised, his hands coming more firmly around me. "You're it."

I tangled my arms around his neck, standing on my tiptoes so I could reach his mouth and he brought his head down, meeting me halfway, and our lips met in a smile. His tongue delicately traced the inside of my mouth and curiosity had me mimic his action, his groan telling me I was doing something right.

Bed? He asked over the bond and I felt a rush of pure happiness at the mental connection we once again shared. He walked me backwards toward the door and I broke off our kiss to stare longingly at the shower. *Next time*, he promised, catching the direction of my gaze.

The back of my legs bumped against the mattress and I fell backwards, enjoying the sensation of the cool, crisp sheets against my naked body. Caleb stood there, his gaze sweeping over me and I could see his jaw tighten when he spotted the bruises. I used my foot to lift the edge of the shirt he still wore and his attention snapped down and I could feel the threadbare control he maintained.

"Take it off," I said sweetly and he yanked it over his head in one smooth motion. His body was strong, capable, and I crawled to my knees to get a closer look, giving in to my desire to explore the dips and curves of muscle and bone.

"You're killing me," he groaned, holding still as I lingered along the plane of his hipbone. The thin sweatpants he wore did little to hide his desire from me and I hooked my fingers on the elastic hem, slowly pulling them down until his dick sprang free, the tip glistening, and moisture pooled at my core. "Dru," I heard the desperation in his voice, the coiled need he barely controlled, and his desire only intensified my own as our emotions spilled into one another over the newly recreated mate link.

I ran my finger over his erection, and his control snapped as he pushed me back on the bed. "My turn," he gritted out roughly, but his touch was impossibly delicate. Each stroke designed to drive me mad as he traced circles around my nipples, watching them pebble but never touching them directly. He continued down and I had to curl my fingers into my palms as he leaned down, his tongue circling my belly button and then dipping inside as his finger found the crease between my legs. I spread my legs further apart as he explored the folds, glossy wetness making his fingers slide with ease as he toyed with the tiny bud exploding with sensation. "Please," I begged, unashamed as my hands came to his shoulders, clawing at him.

He covered me, his dick bumping against my entrance and my insides clenched. He didn't enter me though, his head lowering to my breast, his lips sealing over my erect nipple and he sucked hard as his finger pressed against that bud of nerve endings and I cried out as my world ignited, pleasure burning through me. The rigid length of his dick pressed into me, sending more sparks of pleasure through me as he rubbed against the sensitive bud. I tilted my hips, feeling him sink deeper, and he groaned deep in his throat.

He pulled back, then thrust, and my body felt stretched, almost painfully, but the friction of his thrusts and the tilt of his hips quickly overrode everything else. He quickened his pace, and I could feel the pleasure building inside of him, an echo of my own, and my hand slid to his butt, squeezing in encouragement, needing him to find his release. He thrust faster, hitting my center harder, and I could feel the spiraling need build higher until everything went black as pleasure wiped away every thought, erasing the memory of our broken bond, as we formed a new bond, one that would never be broken.

Chapter Eighteen

Caleb

I watched her sleep, the subtle fringe of her eyelashes hiding those striking mismatched eyes from my view. Contentment filled me, chasing away the last vestiges of restlessness that had consumed me for so long. I stroked the curve of her eyebrow, the color a match to the darker strands of blonde running through her hair. Her scent saturated the air, and I inhaled deeply, picking up the strong note of the earth after a deep rain. She was a perfect mix of wolf and witch, each balancing the other naturally.

Is she awake? Dom's voice intruded in my thoughts and I couldn't help the shortness of my answer.

No.

Wake her up, he ordered and I stiffened at the echo of Alpha command in his words. *This guy you brought back isn't talking and Monster is gone.* Worry seeped through our link and I sat up, realizing something was really wrong if Dom was concerned.

Monster might be out running with Dylan, I replied, seriously hoping that was the case.

No, he never came back. His bed isn't slept in and he's not answering me.

Shit, I murmured, knowing this was bad. If Monster wasn't answering his Alpha then it meant he was too far away or coming way too close to challenging Dom's authority. *Dylan?*

Nothing, but that's not unusual, Dom replied. *Jess is freaking out. She's afraid they went after hunters to find out more about the whole auction thing. I've been trying to get this kid to talk but he's more terrified of your mate than me.*

I almost smiled at the hint of annoyance in Dom's voice at that admittance, but his growing concern overwhelmed me. Monster was headstrong, but he was still young and that combo was enough to get him in trouble. *He might have went to the Ghost Pack*, I mentioned, habit making me use what I now knew was a wildly inaccurate name, and Dom growled.

He better not have, Dom snapped, impotent anger surging through him. *He'll be lucky if I let him run a lap around the school's track if he did.*

I winced at the threat, knowing full well Dom would follow through with it, and there was nothing worse to a wolf than being put on a leash. *I'm sure he didn't*, I replied soothingly, tasting the lie because we both knew full well that was exactly where he'd gone.

He's sixteen, Dom muttered in irritation. *Of course he followed the scent of a female.*

We're on our way, I mumbled hastily, breaking the connection before he turned his aggravation to me. "Dru," I said softly, shaking her shoulder. "We need to get up and go see the others."

Her eyes popped open, the amber and blue of her eyes eerily symmetrical. "Your Pack mates crossed onto our lands," she said, her voice echoing oddly. "Gran isn't happy."

I sighed at having my suspicions confirmed. "We thought so. We're going to get them."

She blinked at me, her hand going to her throat. "Something strange is happening to me," she admitted, sitting up slowly. I wrapped my arm around her, rubbing her back gently. "I have more power than I've ever had. It's right at my fingertips, just waiting to be used."

"You're half witch, half wolf," I commented. "Maybe you're just feeling the witch more now."

"It doesn't feel like half of anything," she replied, exhaling. "Monster didn't listen," she told me, her grimace sympathetic. "But I'm sure Gran will straighten him out."

"That's kind of what I'm afraid of," I answered, getting to my feet. "How did you know?"

"Paige, I think." Dru's nose crinkled. "I was dreaming about her and we were talking."

"You think it was more than a dream?" I questioned and Dru nodded slowly. "That's…different," I settled on, not really sure what to make of this new information and Dru's lips quirked up.

"Different," she breathed with a light chuckle. "Accurate description."

"We need to go. That guy isn't talking and Dom is getting frustrated," I mentioned and her mouth formed an O as she hopped up.

"Damn," she muttered, grabbing the clothes I'd brought her earlier that she'd never had a chance to put on. "Shit," she grumbled as her foot got stuck in her pants leg and I reached over to rescue her, untangling the leg. "Thanks." She yanked her shirt over her head then stared at me, still sitting there bare assed. "Come on. I need to go lift the magic if he's still not able to talk."

I got up, mouthing, "Magic," as I tugged a loose pair of shorts and t-shirt on, catching the door she disappeared through it. "Left," I said as she froze in the hallway. She went left, her hand running along the wall as she stared around in awe. "Straight ahead."

I caught up in time to see her mouth drop open as she entered the kitchen, the huge island sitting square in the middle of the space, and the guy we'd brought back huddled on a bar stool as Dom and Jess's kids brandished plastic swords at him.

He glanced at us in helpless panic, his lips pressed together as Dom stared at him, huge arms crossed over a wide chest, the very picture of intimidating menace. Dru caught sight of him, and as she squinted at the guy, her blue eye glowed faintly. "Speak," she said firmly, and the guy's mouth popped open and he sucked in a deep breath, pathetically grateful as Dom's arms dropped, his stare markedly confused.

"Sorry about that, Luke," Dru said, coming over to stand beside the guy, who was apparently named Luke, and he leaned away from her to my satisfaction. "Are you hungry?" He didn't respond, this time out of sheer terror but it didn't matter because Dru snapped her fingers at Dom. "You have food, big guy?"

A slow blink was the only response she got from the *big guy* and I had to choke back a laugh. One of the kids accidentally poked her in the butt with the plastic sword and she very dramatically cried, "Ouch," covering the spot with her hand as she collapsed against the bar, stating, "I'm mortally wounded." Giggles met her theatrics and I smiled at this unexpected side of her.

Luke eyed her cautiously, some of his fear easing, and Dom relaxed the stick in his ass, as he went to the cabinet and got a handful of beef jerky, tossing it on the bar. Dru's eyes lit up and she grabbed two pieces, one in each hand, as she exclaimed, "I *love* beef jerky."

She turned to Luke, gesturing with one of the sticks of jerky in her hand. "You like beef jerky?" He shrugged uncertainty, but took a piece as she took a bite of hers. "So what do you know about this auction?" She asked, straight to the point and we watched the kid tense. "I'm not going to kill you," she said confidingly. "Neither are they," she added, waving at me and Dom. "But we do need to know. It's kind of a big deal to us if people are selling our kind, ya know?"

He nodded, but didn't speak.

"How about Chuck? What's he know?" My eyebrows came down as she mentioned Chuck and Dom glanced at me. I shrugged, having no idea who he was.

"He's my stepdad," Luke choked out. "He's not nice. I didn't want nothing to do with you children of the night, I swear it."

I winced at his description of us and Dru's mouth pulled to the side. "We're not exactly *children of the night*," she retorted. "Just another species."

"I don't care," he said desperately. "I don't want to be one of you. I don't want nothing to do with any of you. I swear."

"You can't be one of us," she informed him, patting his hand and I growled, feeling the hair on the back of my neck rise. She carefully pulled her hand back as Luke whimpered. "I respect your wishes, but I do need to know what you know before I can let you go."

"Nothing. I swear. He didn't tell me anything. He made me come with him. He didn't tell me what you were or what we were doing with you." His eyes were pleading. "I don't want to hurt anyone. I don't want to be a werewolf."

She smiled tightly, but didn't correct him again. "Did he mention a location or any names? Someone he answered to?" She prodded and Luke shook his head, taking a bite of the jerky.

"Talk to Chuck. He was the one who planned all this. The only guy I met was someone named Strickland. He gave us the wolf," Luke paused, glancing at Dru. "I mean, you, so I guess you know him." She gave him a pained smile and he ducked his head in shame. "I don't know anything else. I swear."

"I believe you, Luke," she said with a sigh. "You didn't actually like Chuck, did you?" She questioned, her mouth making a moue of distaste.

He shook his head, staring at the table. "He married my ma, but he beat her and she died. Then he'd beat me and make me do stuff like this."

"Oh, that's good," Dru replied, a relieved laugh escaping her and Luke's head slowly came up as we all stared at her. "What? He's dead. I'm happy you're not going to be upset about his death," she explained as Dom glanced at me and I lifted my shoulder.

"He's dead," Luke repeated and Dru nodded happily.

"You're welcome."

"What…what am I supposed to do now?" Luke questioned and Dru's eyes narrowed. "I don't have anyone else."

"You're free," Dru told him. "You can do whatever you want."

He stared at her blankly and a sigh gusted from her. "You won't though." She glanced around and shrugged. "You can stay here I guess. If you don't mind children of the night," she offered as her mouth widened in a broad smile, the sight semi terrifying.

"What? No," Dom protested. "No, this isn't a half-way house. You take him."

Dru frowned at him. "You're not very helpful," she told him and I ran my hand over my face to hide my grin.

"I don't want to stay with your kind," Luke complained, eyeing her like she was crazy. "You eat people."

Dru rolled her eyes. "People don't feed a lot. Not enough meat," she confided and Luke looked like he was about to piss himself.

She sounds way too matter of fact, Dom sent over our link and I scratched my eyebrow, not answering.

"How about this? You can go stay with my Gran." She smiled and I recognized it as dangerous, but Luke didn't have a clue. "She hates wolves, so you'll be safe."

Luke nodded slowly. "Okay."

"Great. She can always use a strong pair of arms." Dru stood up, motioning for him to get up. "Let's go."

"Now?" Luke questioned hesitantly and Dru glanced at him in surprise.

"I didn't think you wanted to stay here."

"I don't."

"Plus we need to go get a runaway wolf shifter," she mentioned, nodding to Dom. "You coming?"

"Yes," Dom muttered, trailing behind her as she headed for the door, giving me a pissed off look. "Let's all follow the new girl."

Chapter Nineteen

Dru

As we went outside, the woman who had come with the wolf shifters joined us and I saw the massive mountain of a man lean down to kiss her sweetly. "Dom and his mate, Jess," Caleb explained. "This is their house, those are their kids."

"He's your Alpha."

"Yes."

I nodded at his confirmation as others came up to us. "I don't think we should have a huge crowd," I mentioned as more people continued to gather around and Caleb smiled.

"They won't. They're just curious about you."

I frowned, puzzled. "Me?"

"You're my mate."

"Okaaaay," I drawled, unsure why it mattered. Dom was explaining the situation to Jess as Luke huddled by himself.

"You think bringing him to your Gran is a good idea?" Caleb asked, eyeing him.

"She'll keep him in line," I answered with a shrug. "Or kill him."

"That doesn't bother you?"

"He made his choices, following Chuck even if he didn't agree with him, whatever happens next is up to him," I answered unconcerned. "We should run, it'll be faster."

Dom heard me and gestured to Luke. "He can't run, neither can Jess."

"Then you drive, but we'll run," I replied, not really caring.

Dom looked at Caleb and I suspected they were having a conversation I wasn't privy to. "Annoying, isn't it?" The woman, Jess, said as she came up next to me.

"It is," I replied, glaring at them. "Do they do it a lot?"

"Define a lot."

"Liam will take the Jeep with Jess and Luke," Dom reported, then motioned to me and Caleb. "We'll run ahead, and scout the situation."

"Sounds good," Caleb answered, giving me a look. *I know it's hard, but he is my Alpha, yours too if you join the Pack.*

His words silenced me as I considered the real possibility of finally having a Pack to run with, something that had seemed impossible for so long. The Jeep drove away and the guys started to strip down so I started the shift, not bothering to undress since I didn't know how jealous Caleb might be. Bones cracked, the pain a familiar one, but this time magic raced through me, soothing the pain almost as soon as it presented itself. It was like watching a shift happen in slow motion, except it was me and for the first time, it wasn't an agonizing ordeal.

Dru? Caleb questioned, no doubt sensing my shock.

It didn't hurt, I told him, almost breathless with joy. *It didn't hurt.*

I noticed, he replied, his smile filling my head. *I guess your magic is good for more than levitating.* I felt his puzzlement though as he looked at me. *I thought you were a white wolf.*

I can change my fur to match any color in my hair, I answered, dropping my head in a playful bow. Can't you?

No, he called as I bounded away, taking the lead from Dom, who snapped at my heels, his wolf as massive as the man. *The Alpha usually leads*, Caleb informed me, racing to catch up.

Then he should be faster, I replied carelessly, the feel of earth under my paws giving me speed as instinct guided me home. Both wolves chased after me, but never managed to get closer than the tip of my tail as we ran for the border. *Stay behind me*, I warned as we came closer. *I'll lead you through the traps.*

My words were unnecessary though as we came to border and saw Gran standing there, Paige at her side. Gregory stood there as well, but that wasn't what drew my attention. I shifted to human form, walking slowly to the border, a deep breath filling my lungs as I heard the sweet sound of birds chirping.

"What happened?" I questioned, the words verbal and mental.

Gran smiled, the sight so shocking I blinked. *"You accepted the magic inside of you,"* she answered as Caleb and Dom came up behind me. *"Your mother's magic."*

"*No*," I shook my head, looking to Paige. "*It's yours. The magic goes to you. Not me, I'm a mutant.*"

Gran's mouth pinched regretfully. "*You're not a mutant, Drusilla. Or a freak. You are unique. An amazing gift.*"

"*But I'm a wolf shifter. You hate shifters.*"

"*I admit wolf shifters have taken much from me, but I could never hate you, Dru,*" Gran replied carefully. "*You are my blood. My family and whether you realize it or not, I love every part of you.*"

"*But all this time, you punished me because of the wolf,*" I protested as Caleb took my hand, offering a comfort I didn't know I needed. "*You would starve me, cage me, for what if not because you hated me?*"

"*I wanted you to survive, Drusilla.*" Gran swallowed, her voice thick. "*I knew they would come for you eventually, and all I could do was make sure you were strong enough to survive whatever they would do to you.*" She frowned in remorse. "*My methods might not have been the best.*"

"*You think?*" Caleb commented, drawing her attention. "*And what you did to me? You almost killed Dru.*"

Gran nodded. "*I realized that after the fact. That you had established a mate bond with my granddaughter without my permission. I wondered how you were able to sustain the shifts for so long.*"

"*Why though? Why hurt the shifters who came here?*" I asked, waving my hand. "*What difference did it make?*"

"I was trying to find a way to heal you. I knew what the shift cost you. I thought if I could separate the wolf from the witch then you would be safe. I was wrong," Gran pronounced carefully. *"But in my defense, most of the shifters who came here deserved exactly what they got. They came seeking power, your power, and would have destroyed you to get it."*

I couldn't argue with her, since I knew she was right. There had been more than a few Hanleys and some lone wolves who thought they could take our land and me. Paige darted forward, crossing the border without hesitation and I cried out, *Stop, you'll die.*

No, I won't, Paige promised, her arms coming around me. *You lifted the curse on this land. You accepted the magic into you and now we're all free.*

It was me? I frowned, devastated by the revelation. *"It was always me?"*

"It's not your fault," Gran stated, walking up to us. *"You were a child when your mother died, and her death was something no child should ever have witnessed. You couldn't process it, you rejected the magic you should have inherited. There was nothing I could do but hope eventually you could accept who you were, and the magic that is half of who you are."*

"But why didn't it go to Paige?" I argued. *"She's a true witch."*

"So are you," Gran snapped. *"You adored your father and he encouraged the wolf in you, but neglected the other half of you. Your existence is a beautiful blend of two incredible gifts and that is*

terrifying to some. You are powerful, Dru, and you should never hide that power."

"I thought you hated me because I was a wolf," I murmured and Gran sighed.

"I never hated you. How could I hate someone who reminded me so much of myself?" Gran glanced at my hand entwined with Caleb's and bit her lip. *"I only wanted you to be happy. Happy in your own skin and to not feel the need to hide who you were. I didn't want you to make the same mistakes I made."* She looked at Caleb, her lips pursuing. *"Perhaps, you chose better than I did. He's certainly stubborn enough."*

"Will you give us your blessing?" I asked boldly and she stared at me for a second, her mouth twisting as she gave me a short nod. *"Thank you."*

"It's time I let the past go too," she admitted, her gaze straying to Gregory. Paige clapped, startling us, as she glanced around, her smile brighter than the sun.

I love a happy ending, she sighed, clasping her hands.

"Where's Monster?" Dom interrupted, not hearing Paige, his gaze impatient as it swept the clearing. "You better not have hurt my wife's little brother because I do not want to hear about that shit for the next twenty years," he added, pointing his finger and Gran's mouth drew up.

"You better put that finger down before I break it," she ordered and he lowered his hand, drawing back warily. "Your brother is fine."

"Brother in law," Dom corrected, glancing around. "Then where is he?"

"I'm here," Monster answered sheepishly, stepping from the cover of the trees. "I showed up, ready to rescue Paige from her Gran, but it wasn't necessary."

Gran is going to let me come stay with you, Paige told me excitedly, almost bouncing. *Monster was telling me about high school. It's real, Dru. Not just in books.*

"I think she's a little old for high school," Caleb said out of the corner of his mouth and I shrugged.

"What difference does it make? Do they kick you out if you're too old?" I asked and he shook his head as he answered, "No, we can fudge her age if necessary." I nodded crisply as Dom stared at us in confusion.

Is this what you want, Paige? To come and stay in a house with me? Go to school? I wanted to make sure it was what Paige wanted and not what I wanted for her, but I wasn't above bribery either. *They have hot showers and washing machines.*

Paige's eyes rounded as she squealed. *Yes, it's everything I want. He can hear me,* Paige confided, her gaze darting to Monster. *I like talking to him.*

I'm glad, I told her as Caleb suddenly smirked, his gaze going to Dom.

"Oh, you've got to be kidding me," Dom burst out, pacing away from us as he ran his hands through his black hair, those yellow eyes glaring at nothing. "I'm not ready for this." He waved his hand between Monster and Paige. "No mating until you're both out of the damn house." He shook his head. "Thomas is going to kill me. He leaves for two weeks and now his son is in love." He grimaced. "With a witch." He dropped his hands. "Just shoot me now."

Gran smiled as she said, "I can arrange that."

Caleb's story was a difficult one to write. It took me months longer than I thought it would and it changed a dozen times in the process, but I love Caleb and Dru together, and hope I did their story justice. There's just something about alpha males and wolf shifters that I have always loved. Originally, I never intended to write Caleb's story, but it kept nagging at me, an unfinished thread, a boy Alpha that needed time to grow up and redeem himself. I feel he did just that and with Dru by his side, I imagine there's nothing they can't accomplish. Now, Monster....he's a whole different story.

If you want to see what's coming next, check out my Facebook page, Kristin Coley Author, or my website, www.kristincoley.com, once there you can always click the link and sign up for my newsletter if you prefer. I love to hear from readers and reviews are always welcome. Reviews help readers find new authors and if you have an extra minute I'd love if you could leave one.

Happy reading,
Kristin